This first edition of "The Ephemera"
is limited to twenty-six signed and
lettered editions.

This is copy F

~ The A-Z of Ephemera ~

F is for Fortune, Fame, and
Fifteen minutes

The Ephemera

The Ephemera

stories

Neil Williamson

LASTIC
PRESS

Printed by MRT Response, Bristol, UK

Cover design by Gregor Scharff
Cover layout by Dean Harkness
Typeset by Marie O'Regan

Published by:
Elastic Press
85 Gertrude Road
Norwich
UK

elasticpress@elasticpress.com
www.elasticpress.com

For Kitty, who I love for all the little things she does.

And for my parents, Norman and Raena, who have always provided constancy and encouragement.

Acknowledgements

This collection would not have been possible without the help of a large number of people, for which I am grateful.

Firstly to Andrew Hook whose dedication to the short story deserves more awards than it is possible to bestow. And to John Jarrold for his legendary enthusiasm and support.

To the editors: Erich Zahn, Andy Cox, David Pringle, Keith Brooke, John Benson, DF Lewis, John Klima, John Navroth, Marie O'Regan, Paul Kane, Trevor Denyer, Andrew J Wilson and the Albedo cabal.

To Mark Roberts, who shares the byline and the blame for one of the stories included here. At least half of every word and idea is his. Thanks, mate.

To Jeff Vandermeer, Liz Williams and Tamar Yellin for their friendship and advice. And to all of Storyville.

And lastly to the sharpest bunch of critiquers and friends there is, the Glasgow SF Writers Circle: Duncan Lunan, Phil Raines, Al Duncan, Gary Gibson, Craig Marnoch, Mike Cobley, Paul Cockburn, Elsie Donald, Jim Steel, Lawrence Osborn, Jim Campbell, Daniel Livingstone, Jamie McLean, Mike Gallacher, Richard Mosses, Eliza Chan, Cynthia Smith, Lori (and John) Martin, Andy Nimmo, Ria Cheyne, Barrie Condon, Veronica Colin, Richard Hammersley, Graeme Gardner, Jim Whyte, Irene Gordon, Roddy Chisholm and all of the others that have taken part over the years. Thanks to you all for lasting the course, and being the least ephemeral people I know.

Table of contents

Shine, Alone After The Setting Of The Sun 9

The Euonymist 21

The Bone Farmer 37

The Happy Gang 57

Cages 71

Amber Rain 79

Postcards 93

Softly Under Glass 107

Well Tempered 121

Harrowfield 127

The Apparatus 151

The Bennie and The Bonobo 159

A Horse In Drifting Light 171

Sins of the Father 177

Hard To Do 197

The Codsman and His Willing Shag 203

Shine, Alone After The Setting Of The Sun

When I got home from the studio Annie was smashing crockery on the back step. I laid my guitar case down and watched my lover standing at the kitchen door, silvered by the 2am moonlight, dropping mugs and plates and breakfast bowls one at a time onto the concrete. From the living room, drifting jungle noises and David Attenborough's sonorous murmur counterpointed the explosive shattering.

"*Annie!*" I yelled.

She turned and grinned breezily. "Hi, Lorna. You're back. How was the session?"

I was amazed. When I left that morning, she hadn't even seemed aware that I was going out.

"What are you doing?"

At least she had the grace to look abashed. "Oh, right. Bit of a guddle, yeah?" Then she actually beamed. "I'm getting back to work."

I watched her as she crouched and began to sort through the mess of fragments. Such a transformation. Right up to that morning she had been so withdrawn, so tightly, bitterly wound, self-exiled to her own dark, curtains-drawn world, doing nothing except sleep and watch her nature videos; and now everything about her seemed to deny the last few months had happened. The brightness of her expression; the renewed energy in her step; the almost forgotten spark of drive in her eyes, replacing that smudged, haunted cast. All this spoke of some remarkable, but so welcome, return of normalcy, of the Annie I knew and loved and had wanted back for so long.

But... however much I wanted to believe this, however much I found myself grinning too, infected by whatever inspiration had sparked this shift of mood, I was equally fearful that it signified some darker, internalising twist of Annie's psyche. I knew her too well.

Right at that moment, though, I was tired and my head was too full of the day's jingles to tackle the problem. I mumbled something like *okay then*, and went to run myself a bath.

*

Annie was sitting on the step, carefully breaking up the larger pieces with pliers. I came to stand behind her, feeling soft and renewed. Without turning, she said, "You smell of apples."

I ran my fingers through thick strands of damp hair. "I borrowed your shampoo. Sorry."

She gave me no sign, and I could read nothing in the curve of her spine under her thin, stretched *Greenpeace* t-shirt as she bent over her work, so I took a chance. Slowly, braced for rejection, I lowered myself to the floor behind her, wrapping my arms and legs around, resting my head on a shoulder, breathing in warm body scent, relishing the proximity. And Annie responded, laying down her pliers, leaning back and relaxing into my embrace.

We sat like that in a silence I was powerless to break until the weight of questions finally forced words from my lips.

"How are you?" Weak, insipid, open to as non-committal a reply as you could get. At first it seemed that Annie was not going to give even that, but then she spoke.

"I'm all right I suppose. I wake up every morning hating myself for bringing a child into this world and go to sleep hating myself double for not being able to do anything to make it better."

Straight to the point; and it told me that not everything had changed. Annie had been running this conviction around since she discovered she was pregnant, digging it deeper, etching out the grooves of it in her mind. How many times had I tried to reason her out of this and met with violent rejection, or with that blank silence, so intense, which I found even scarier? That was before. Maybe now she would listen. My fingers described light, calming circles on her brow as I searched for some new combination of words that would convince her.

"The world's not all so terrible, you know." I said it lightly, but Annie twisted round fast, fixing me with a hot stare that dried everything I was going to say to dust in my mouth. Her stare softened, her eyes brimming and spilling twin tracks down her cheeks as she reached up to shush me with one finger, one shake of the head. I felt the tension drain from her, and her body sagged against me, head resting this time on my shoulder. My fingers resumed their tiny movements at her brow and in her thick hair. Quietly, into my chest, she said,

"All I wish is that we could have our own little corner where everything is good and safe and just right for us."

"People like you make the world better, Annie." It was feeble but Annie seemed to take a measure of comfort from it, cuddled in a little closer, squeezed my arm lightly. I was grateful for that at least. I didn't even mind the heavy press of her belly against my leg. Presently a growing coolness in the air set us both shivering and I coaxed her to stand and come inside, asking, "What *are* you doing out here anyway?" For the third time that night, she

11

smiled, and that one was genuine, one hundred per cent Annie.

"I have to make a mosaic. For the baby."

*

When it came to her work, everything was *must*, or *need*, or *have to* with Annie. Each of her paintings, once she latched onto an idea, was driven to completion by some inner force; usually at the neglect of those around her. That was just her way. She might scratch around for ages for a concept, but once she had it she became fixated and worked hard at it until it was done. It was a fascinating, entertaining process to watch; perilous if you got too close, and often lonely for the observer.

At the end of it though, without fail, something special. A lurid scene, a slant-wise look at the world centred around one or more of Annie's characteristic elongated figures, stylised people simplified to bright ribbons. She said they were human beings reduced to spiritual essence. *String people*, was how I thought of them.

Annie's String People pictures just about sold, eventually. Sometimes for more, usually for less, but at least they sold. And she had managed to produce them at more or less regular intervals over a couple of years. Money came in, but her contribution to our finances was small compared to mine. Certainly I envied her. I'd have loved to sit and write songs all day instead of tossing off standards and carpet warehouse jingles for take after incomplete take as some idiot drummer slowly got his act together, but any resentment I felt was swept aside by my regard for her talent. I loved each one of those pictures, marvelled at the fierce intensity of colour she favoured. They moved me, and I found them attractive and repellent in equal measure. I couldn't wait until a new one was completed.

Of course, Annie had done nothing recently. No paintings, no sketches. Since discovering her pregnancy she had been unable to work. For weeks she had fidgeted around at her board. Then in her frustration she turned to other forms, other media. Still nothing. Nada. Zilch. Now, suddenly, this mosaic.

*

Annie made herself a rectangular frame which covered most of the kitchen floor. She sat before it cross-legged, surrounded by a semicircle of Tupperware tubs, each containing a pile of pieces; clay, porcelain, metal, glass. I stepped around her to get to the kettle for coffee, watching as she carefully chose a piece, shaped it with a file, cemented it and found a place for it. Rather than the geometric elements traditional in mosaic design, Annie's pieces were shaped irregularly, their edges smoothed and curved to fit with their neighbours. Each had their chosen place in a pattern which was building inwards from the edges of the frame. Perhaps, though, *pattern* was the wrong word. Certainly, I could not yet identify any form emerging from this pebbled pixel-array. That was the impression it gave, a blankness, like the static on an untuned TV.

*

Annie went out in the car. She left before I woke, and was gone maybe a couple of hours. Just enough time for me to start worrying; and get pissed at her for making me worry. She had not set foot outside the house in over three weeks. I had just decided to start ringing round when she walked into the house, her arms laden with plants in clay pots. Even more filled the boot of the car. An eclectic collection of flowers, shrubs and vegetable plants, one or two of each, even a couple of bonsais. I sighed, mystified. Annie had never been a gardener.

    I helped her to unload the car. Neither of us spoke but I caught Annie's eye, asking wordlessly, *Why?* The reply was that cheeky, knowing look that she was so good at. *Because*. And I

13

smiled, just a little.

Over lunch our conversation was light, inconsequential. I found that I was beginning to believe this return to as normal a life as you could expect with Annie, however suddenly it might have come about. It was seductive. I wanted it badly, but was afraid to surrender to it completely.

*

The plant pots all found their way into the mosaic. Fragments of them anyway. When I came home that evening there was a broad band of terracotta across the picture, and a heap of dark earth and discarded plants outside the door.

"Oh Jesus, Annie. This is too much," I said to myself, because at that moment there was no sign of her. Then footsteps sounded behind me and I turned, too fast, propelled by anger. Annie shrieked, jumped back, losing her grip on the glass of water in her hand. The tumbler shattered on the concrete. Water, icy, clear, splashed my feet, dribbling in amongst the earth, pooling muddily around my shoes.

"Ah shit," I cursed, stepping away. She went and spent all that money on plants and now this. "Annie,..." I began, but I ran out of words.

Annie's face had gone tight, shrunk inwards, an expression somewhere between hurt and defiance. She spoke quietly, but with venom, "*Okay.* I was just coming out to clean this stuff up. I thought we could plant them in the garden. It *is* summer after all."

My anger melted away into... what? Pity, sympathy, confusion? "Yeah, look, I'll give you a hand."

"Thanks," Annie's face cracked weakly, an attempt at a smile.

Little things like shared tasks, working away without the need for conversation, are what I loved about our relationship. Just being there with her, breathing her air, sharing her with no-one. Occasionally I sneaked glances at her, admired her single minded attention to trowel and earth, to stem and woody roots. The same as when I watched her in her studio; just standing, looking on as she went about her work. Never once did I catch her glancing back at me, but I didn't mind.

Later she picked up the pieces of broken tumbler, delicately disposing of the shards. The thick round base she kept though. Something about it fascinated her. She held it in her palm, traced its still wet surface with a careful, deliberate finger. Then, with a secret little smile, she took it inside.

*

"*Hey*! What's all this?"

Annie looked up from attending to the steaming array of ironware on the hob. Big smile, warm and generous.

"Hi. Sit down, it's nearly ready."

I stepped nimbly around the mosaic to reach the table, used to it being there now, a part of the kitchen; even if it still refused to offer me anything resembling a recognisable picture.

The table was set with plates that did not match, and a bottle of red wine had been opened and placed in the centre of the table beside a pair of candles which were slender and white as bone.

I sat, poured myself a glass. The wine was thin, but I savoured it.

"So candles, wine. You cooking dinner. What's the big occasion?"

"Celebration," Annie said, placing a bowl of potatoes before me. "I've nearly finished the mosaic and you're going to have a weekend at the seaside."

I took another swallow of wine to disguise my surprise, and disappointment. As far as I could see, the mosaic was a mess. Still, Annie seemed to be bursting with pride over it. Maybe this was a practice piece. Perhaps it would take her a while to regain, or redefine, her style.

Neil Williamson

"What are you talking about? I'm not going anywhere."

"Yes you are. Bob rang today. They need a guitarist for a week down at the Pavilion. Starting tomorrow night. I said you'd do it. We need the money."

"No, Annie. Money's not that tight. I need to be here with you."

Annie came over, took my hand. "It's okay. *I'm* okay, honest."

Her expression was so open. In it I read understanding and gratitude and love. "Listen, I've not been that easy to live with recently. I know that. I'm sorry and I'm so grateful that you stayed around. I was so worried that Sam would, you know ... come between us." Her left hand drifted absently to the pronounced swell of her belly.

Sam? Had she named her child already? That would be just like her. Shaping it before it was even born. Or was she referring for the first time to the father. We had never talked about that. By rights I suppose I should have been the one throwing tantrums, sick with jealousy that she had been with someone else, a man; that I wasn't enough for her. But I knew that anyway. I accepted long ago that Annie's life did not revolve around me as mine did around her. When she came home one day, mad as hell and told me she was pregnant, I hurt, sure, but Annie's need was greater than mine. The state she was in, I knew I would have to be there for her. She offered no apology, no explanation. I told myself that I didn't really expect any.

I said, "Annie, no..." meaning to stop her. If she was going to explain now I didn't want to hear the details of who and where and why. She ignored the interruption.

"I'm glad he hasn't. I think you do need a bit of time away though, away from this house anyway."

I suddenly liked the idea, but not just for myself. "We could both go. The seaside would do you good. The fresh air..."

"No." Annie cut me off sharply. "I need to finish the mosaic."

16

She shrugged. "You know how I am. When you come back, we'll go somewhere."

It was there in those big, beautiful, too idealistic eyes. I should have seen it, but I didn't. Not then.

"Somewhere really nice. Together. I promise."

I allowed myself to be persuaded. "Okay, I'll go. Thanks, love."

*

Later, Annie was staring at me through the green glass of the empty wine bottle. Slow wax dribbled down the side from the candle wedged into the neck. I leaned back in my chair, strumming loose chords, warm sixths and sevenths, on my old acoustic. Dreamily Annie reached out, her fingers resting lightly on the glass. She spoke softly, her voice muted by the wine.

"I can feel every note you play. Vibrating. Your music is so beautiful, but it lasts so short a time."

I put the guitar down and went over to her, touching her hair.

"Come on," I said. "Let's go to bed."

Lying together, relishing every warm point of contact between us. So good to return to this at last. So good to have the old Annie back. As I drifted into sleep Annie whispered into my spine.

"You will bring your music back to me, Lorna, won't you?"

"Of course."

"I couldn't live without your music."

"I love you too, Annie."

*

As soon as I opened the door I knew Annie was gone. The house sighed its emptiness. Crossing the threshold, I stepped into a calmness, as if a great tension, invisible until now, had been

17

released. It was the relief of looking up at the inky-black, star-pocked sky after a long day under a fierce, unrelenting sun.

The TV drew my attention first. For weeks it had been on constantly in the background, showing Annie's videos of nature programmes, and now it was conspicuous by its silence. Easy to see why. Its screen had been caved in, spilling dead-grey chunks of glass onto the carpet. There was more. The bedroom mirror had suffered similar vandalism; and around the house various other items had been smashed or broken.

In the kitchen, the late evening sun illuminated a wedge of floor; a hot knife blade of light slicing across Annie's mosaic. Now, at last, I could see the picture. Why only now? Tears blurred my vision as I began to understand the sense of it, as if my body was trying to blind me even at this late stage.

A scene; so real, so clever. I could almost feel the warmth of the clay road beneath the naked soles of my feet, baked by the polished copper disc of the sun. To the sides of the road, smudged greenery was beginning to sprout from the dark earth, and in the distance a smoky grey forest, restless with quick shadows that echoed with the calls of exotic birds and animals. Off to one side, a cold lake, still and clear as glass, invited me to drink.

In the centre, at the focus of the piece, two of Annie's string people, one long and one short. Two thin strands composed from slices of silvered glass, shining with the sun's white-yellow brilliance. I let my fingers trace the strips of warm glass thoughtfully, then the aperture beside the figures, a dark hole similar to them in shape. The only piece of the mosaic that remained to be completed.

Annie had left a note. It lay on the table weighed down by the empty wine bottle from that last meal and a hand-sized rectangular mirror which reflected my face. Not pretty. Puffy, dewy eyes betrayed my feelings, but there was no-one there to see them. The handwriting was neat, almost childlike. As was her way, it said very little, and it spoke volumes.

Shine, Alone After The Setting Of The Sun

Sorry Lorna. So beautiful, couldn't wait. A

First I swept up the broken things around the house, and then tidied up in general, washing and scrubbing, brushing, polishing. *Erasing*. Then, when the house was a place I felt I could live in normally again, I went to the step and broke the glass, selecting appropriate pieces and tidying the rest into the bin. In the kitchen I cemented the pieces into the place reserved for them. They glowed in the sunlight as if lit from the inside; a soulful, bottle green, so deep I could almost hear captured chords strummed softly on an old guitar, remembered music rising with the heat in the shimmering air, echoing far across the lake. And yes, I thought, it *was* beautiful.

I took pride in that thought. With night falling I grabbed my guitar and went to sit on the step. Sitting under the stars, my seat still surrounded by splinters of glass and china and clay, I rediscovered chords and melodies. I sat and sang all my old songs until they were exhausted, and then, remembering how, I started to make a new one. In it, I wished Annie and the baby well, wherever they were, and then, after that, I just played for the pleasure of playing for myself.

The Euonymist

Calum knew there was a word for it. This sick feeling that had been accreting stealthily in his gut since the transport burned down from the orbital and lit in over the North Atlantic; that had formed a discernable kernel over Arran and bubbled up to his chest when they landed. When he set foot on Scottish tarmac again, he felt it tickle his heart in a most unwelcome way. It was like anticipation of something you knew you should be looking forward to but suspected might not turn out the way you wanted at all. Anticipation, yes, and there was an element of leaden fatigue to it too. There was definitely a word. Calum pondered it as the government car shushed him southwards out of Prestwick on the rain-glittered expressway heading down the Ayrshire coast. If anyone should have been able to come up with the name of this feeling, it should have been him but, even with the implants off, his head was still mired in the Lexicon mindset. None of the words that came to him out of the residuals created in his flesh brain by the thousand-language database were quite right.

It was a human feeling. It needed a human word. He was sure it would come to him in time. Now that he was home.

Scotland in July. The lazy, wheeling polka of sun and rain, baking the earth to oven stillness before dousing it with steaming flash showers. Chasing the clouds down past Ayr, heading inland via Maybole, the car's windows were slapped with wet foliage so lush and luminous green that for a disorientating moment Calum could have been back in Ghessareen's island jungles. To stop from thinking about that he mouthed the names of the roadside plants to himself – the thick ferns, the wide-leafed sycamores and chestnuts, the tall, purple foxgloves springing erect, relieved of their burden of water by the car's passing. Calum enjoyed the foursquare precision of the Latin, the quirky, old folksiness of the English. On Ghessareen nothing had a name until he had given it one. Here, it had all been done centuries ago. *Foxglove*, he thought. Whoever it had been that came up with that, they had a sure gift for euonymy. The name fit perfectly. Of course it had originally been 'folk's glove', but whoever had decided that the little bell-shaped blossoms might have been used as faerie mittens had created a lasting image. Calum sometimes wondered what it would have been like if the Unification Bloc had come here before humans had evolved language. What would a foxglove have been called then? If the influence of the Integrated Machine Intelligences had been ascendant at that point it would have been something horribly functional like, 'flowering-plant-of-average-height:0.7m-with-many-blossoms-of-hue:400nm-wavelength'. Thank Christ Earth had been overlooked for long enough for uniquely imaginative names like foxglove to rise up, get spread around, and achieve acceptance through established use and their own organic rightness.

"Foxglove." He said it aloud, and the unnamed feeling receded.

*

Calum looked into the baby's eyes once more, just to be sure. The infant gazed up, yawned in a way that suggested the serenity she had displayed for the last five minutes was about to slip into boredom. He took it as a warning sign. He'd had her long enough anyway.

When Calum opened the door the expectant *sotto voce* murmur stilled, and the faces of thirty or so assorted family, extended family and close friends and neighbours all turned his way. En masse they leaned forward an inch or two. The youthful mother — his cousin Donna, who had barely started secondary school when Calum had left Earth – and her equally callow boyfriend beamed like idiots. This was almost as stressful as reporting a naming judgement to the Bloc.

"She looks to me," he said, "like an Ellen."

There was a pause before the predictable chorus of *oohs* came, followed by a smattering of applause. It had been just a hint of a pause, but it was a familiar one to Calum and it brought the feeling back with a vengeance. It was the pause that happened when no-one wanted to react to a new name until they found out what the person it mattered most to thought. A grimace of consternation passed across the baby's features. It matched the look on her mother's face. Calum decided it was a good time to reunite them.

"There you go," he said. "Congratulations."

Donna offered a niggardly smile. "Thanks."

As if seeking to head off an onrushing display of petulant ingratitude, Calum's always harmonious Uncle Dan wedged himself into the picture.

"Well done, Calum, son." He pumped Calum's hand. "We're very grateful." His eyes widened. "*Honoured*, even."

Neil Williamson

"There's no need really," Calum murmured. "For the family, it's a pleasure."

Through the resuming chatter, and the baby's precursory whimpers, Calum heard Donna whine peevishly to her mother. He matched Uncle Dan's fixed grin with one of his own.

"Honoured," Dan repeated. "That a famous... er..."

"Euonymist," Calum supplied.

"Darling, you can always use it as a middle name." The whole room must have heard his Aunt Geraldine's whisper. The volume of conversation swelled with shared discomfort.

"...a famous *unanimist*..." Dan attempted gamely.

"Something classy, I agree..." Geraldine soothed.

"...should do us the honour of naming our wee Ellen."

"*Shaz-nay!*" bellowed Donna. "Her name's Shaznay!"

The feeling that Calum had been unable to name filled him completely. The heavy anticipation had blossomed into resigned embarrassment, and in its wake came that universal certainty of not being able to please all of the people all of the time. And by the way the rest of the onlookers were guzzling their drinks and inspecting the contents of their paper plates he suspected that they shared some of what he felt. He wondered if any of them knew what the feeling was called.

Calum looked around for a diversion, but no-one was helping him out on this one. Even his mum had vanished. Then an unlikely escape route appeared, and it came in the form of an old woman rearing up unsteadily off of one of the kitchen chairs that had been set out to provide extra seating. It was the dress Calum recognised. It was a violently puce floral affair that did nothing to disguise Auntie Bella's uncertain shape – a morphology of bone curvature and body fat redistribution peculiar to Scottish grande dames that Calum had long suspected was due to the accretion of density through years of accumulated nicotine, sarcasm and fried potato scones. It hadn't happened yet, but with the increased longevity treatments coming out of Earth's trade with the Bloc it was surely only a matter of time before the first

24

Scottish granny turned herself inside out and ended up as a kind of greasy black hole. All that would be left would be a set of false teeth, a pair of wrinkly tights and a box of After Eight mints filled with empty wrappers.

"Whit's he cried the bairn then?" Auntie Bella's croaky caw had once engendered terror in all of Calum's cousins, seeing as it was usually followed by a smack on the legs or, worse, a flabby kiss. Now, however, it was more than welcome.

"She's called Shaznay." Donna's tone defied anyone to disagree.

Bella wobbled closer, peered at the increasingly fractious infant. "Shaznay?" she said. "Whit's that, Shaznay? Wha's cried Shaznay? Lookit thon face? Dis that resemmle a Shaznay to you?"

"Actually, the name was Ellen." Calum's mother had reappeared at the living room door. Better late than never. He made a mental note to thank her for her support later.

Bella regarded the baby again. "Aye, Ellen'd be fair eneuch, hen. Yer mither's got a second cuisin in Canada cawd Ellen."

"I have?" said a surprised Geraldine.

At that moment baby Shaznay/Ellen, or whatever she would eventually be known as when she was old enough to choose for herself, decided that enough was enough and began to scream.

"Aye, and she was a greeter an aw," finished Bella, turning her attention to a plate of hot sausage rolls.

*

Calum sat on the garden bench with his mother. Even at the end of the long-stretched summer evening, with the stars beginning to show in the deepening sky, it was still quite warm enough to sit out. If you didn't mind the midges. A cloud of them spun like a slow tornado around the nearby flowerbeds. There was another perfect euonym. The word just encapsulated the infuriating quality of the tiny insect; and it could be utilised as satisfying invective if the need arose.

"Midges." Calum smiled, then slapped his hand against his arm. "Wee bastards."

His mother smiled with him. "Thanks for doing that today," she said. "Pay no mind to Geraldine and Donna. They may not stick with the name you gave them, but they'll take the prestige that comes with it."

Calum shrugged. "I name planets for a living. What did they expect?"

The midge-cloud had gyrated above the roses, lingering there over the creamy, pinky, yellowy blossoms. Strange behaviour. Usually they headed straight for him, but he'd only been pestered by a couple of stray ones so far. Something about the rosebeds was apparently more interesting than him tonight. He wondered if it was the perfume. Did midges have a sense of smell, or was that the insects on Yrrow he was thinking of?

"You were the model of diplomacy," his mother said.

Calum laughed. "I've played to tougher audiences."

"You always had a way with words, though. Ever since..."

"Ever since I was four years old, when I looked at myself in the mirror for a whole hour and then told you I wasn't to be called Brian any more because my name should really be Calum. I remember."

"And when we told you not to be so silly, you screamed the place down."

The midges had moved on to the big rhododendron in the garden's back corner. His mother got up from the bench and approached the roses, slipping a pair of secateurs out of her cardigan pocket as she knelt by the bed. "I hope young Shaznay has a similar moment of self determination when she... oh."

"What is it?" When his mother didn't answer Calum went over to find out.

"I don't know," she said. "I've never seen anything like this before." She leant back to let him see.

At first Calum thought it was just a stray shoot. Some sort of weed, no more than three inches tall, dwarfed among the tall rose stems, but with spiky looking stiletto leaves to rival its neighbours' thorns. Then he saw the way it gleamed in the last of the sunlight, flaky amber on silver like rusted steel.

His insides lurched. He had a very bad feeling about this. Much worse than the unnamed one. This one was the cast-iron cannonball of dread.

*

When Calum came back into the house his mother had turned the kitchen into a research centre. A stack of discarded gardening books surrounded her at the table where she had unrolled a screen and an interface to search the web for more exotic specimens. She tapped awkwardly at the flat keyboard. The lacerated gardening glove and blunted secateurs lay beside the screen. The end of her bandaged thumb was turning pink again.

"Nothing yet?" Calum asked, in hope rather than expectation. He wanted her to find it, but he was becoming increasingly certain that she would not. Not a viciously bladed bio-metallic organism like that. Not in all the botanical lists on this Earth. He sneaked a glance at the readout of his analyser. *Please wait*, it read. It would take longer to consult the vast botanical databases of the Bloc, of course, and while discovering a known extro species in his mum's back garden carried with it a number of unpleasant implications, it would still be preferable to it not finding anything at all. He hadn't turned on the Lexicon implants. That would come later, when all else had failed.

Calum looked out the window. It was too dark to see it now, but he could feel it out there, a problem growing with every minute that passed. It hadn't been there when his mother had been out that afternoon shortly before he arrived, she had assured him – and he believed her, gardeners had an eye for these things – which meant that it had grown four inches in a few hours. Which really wasn't a good thing at all.

Calum checked his analyser before he went to bed. *Please*

wait. He knew he didn't have to wait. He was pretty sure what the answer would be anyway, so he could act now – *should* act now – but given the option, he waited.

*

They started arriving not long after dawn. Calum woke to a gabble of voices, the kind of squabble that universally signified opposing vested interests. He checked his watch, his phone, the analyser: 05:12, seven missed calls, *No species match.* The unnamed feeling woke too. It shifted inside him like slipping sand.

Calum got up, pulled on some clothes, then, reluctantly, sub-voxed a command that engaged the Lexicon implants.

The scene in the kitchen was chaotic. An auditory nightmare that his translator implants would have approached melt-down to make sense of. Fortunately, he had neglected to turn them on as well. Best just to leave it that way for now. That the majority of the yabbering occupants were human was something of a relief, but Calum immediately spotted representatives of at least three other Bloc races. A Peloquin pair were haranguing a black woman with a placatory attitude and a very expensive-looking suit. Earth-Bloc liaison, Calum decided. She could handle it. A breeze of movement and a purplish blur in the air told him there were Tage here too. He unfocussed his gaze for a moment and saw it clearer, a vague indigo outline. A noise like a jar of wasps – a *big* jar. It was agitated about something. Calum shrugged, tapped his ear to show he didn't understand, and the Tage buzzed angrily and moved on. The third species he recognised was a tall, butter-skinned Uidean. That was encouraging. If this panned out like he feared, Earth was going to need all of their friends on side. For now though the unfortunate sod had been cornered by Aunt Bella.

"Is sumbdy puttin the kettle on or no? I'm awfy drouthie, so I am," she told it.

The confused-looking extro was tapping the side of his head nervously, but Aunt Bella didn't seem to understand the signal.

28

Calum thought about rescuing it, but the Uideans were seasoned diplomats. They'd surely faced worse – though perhaps not stranger – than Bella. Besides, there was activity in the garden that demanded his attendance.

There were maybe half a dozen people standing around – or in – the rosebed, which itself was now covered in an open tent of heavy plastic sheeting. Calum's mother stood to one side in her dressing gown and slippers talking to a rumpled-looking man in a hairy suit. Calum would have recognised his boss from his posture alone.

"Good to see you, Clarence," he said. From the centre of the group clustered around the roses came sounds of exertion and a metallic grating that made Calum think of sharpening knives.

Sneijder turned. He didn't look happy, but then he rarely did. "You should have notified us."

"I followed procedure," Calum replied calmly. "Species discovered in pre-nomenclatured areas have to be cross-referenced with both local and Lexicon lists."

The Dutchman's lip curled. "Calum, you understand, don't you, the implications if this turns out to be a completely new species? You should have notified us straight away. God, for containment and assessment, if nothing else."

Calum felt the feeling shift inside him again. He could almost hear the sighing of the slipping sand. One of the workers stepped to the side, revealing that the plant had already erupted into a dense bush as tall as his chest, sprouting fists of blade-leaves in all directions. One of the other workers did something that set the whole thing quivering with a noise like an emptied cutlery drawer. "*Bloody... thing*," the worker tailed off, at a loss for a suitable epithet. Then, examining his steel mail gloves for damage, he told someone to *fetch the torch*.

"All the more reason for following procedure," Calum told Sneijder. "Given the political ramifications, they will be examining every step of the process. We've got to be above board all the way." This was true, but what was truer was that he'd suspected that he knew what was going on from the moment he saw the plant, and he'd wanted to postpone all of this as long as possible. If there was a contamination risk, the botanical one at least wasn't unmanageable. At least he'd got a decent night's sleep out of it.

"All right, what's done is done," Sneijder came closer. "But I need to ask you about Ghessareen."

Calum had thought he might. "What about it?"

"Well, specifically the quarantine procedures?" Sneijder said. "Is there any chance at all..."

"That I could have brought something back with me?" Calum sighed. "Well, let's see. They pulled us off Ghessareen with the job half done and no explanation, and replaced us with an inexperienced team of Bellussibellom. Then they quibbled over virtually every item in our necessarily incomplete report, rendering any information about any of the catalogued species confused to the point of useless. And even though they made us go through the decontamination procedure three times before they let us leave the station, virtually everything on the Ghessareen orbital just happened to be glitching from a suspected virus that they never did track down. So, in short, yes, it's possible that I brought something back with me that wasn't killed dead like it should have been. It would certainly be one explanation for how this thing ended up in my mother's garden."

Sneijder's nose wrinkled in disgust. He might have known what the problem was with the Ghessareen survey, but he wasn't telling.

Calum wasn't going to let being kept in the dark about it upset him. "Look there are plants not a million miles away from this in the northern archipelagos. Similar, but not the same. The plants that grow on Ghessareen wouldn't survive our alkali soil, let alone flourish like this. This is totally new." He looked at Sneijder to see if he had caught the subtext.

The Dutchman arched a bushy brow, lowered his voice. "Mutation?"

"Almost certainly."

"Natural or engineered."

"I'm not a botanist, Clarence, but given the source of the naming assignation that we used on Ghessareen..."

"I'm not going to like this, am I?"

"Peloquin."

"Fuck," Sneijder spat. "Fuck, fuck, fuck! I thought they were pretty quick to get out here."

"Exactly." This time Sneijder sighed with him.

"I'm going to have to get guidance from the diplomats on this," he said at length. "I shouldn't do this because of your involvement, but none of the others can get here sooner than a week, so I'm officially appointing you the case euonymist. But do me a favour. Don't go making any promises until you hear from me."

"No fear on that score," Calum said. "I'm going back to bed."

*

It turned out to be the best thing he could have done. Not only did it give him the chance to rest, but it also insulated him from having to actually interact with the various Bloc representatives who were still crowding the house. He didn't sleep, just lay there in the darkened room, staring at what had been his childhood bedroom walls. Beside the closet there had been an RSPB poster showing a montage of British garden birds, and he had memorised every one of them by the age of ten, spellbound by the names. *Finches: chaffinch, bullfinch, goldfinch, greenfinch, crossbill, linnet, yellowhammer... Yellowhammer.* There was a euonym if ever there was one. Surrounded by names like those it was little wonder that he'd found himself suited to a career in euonymy. If only there had turned out to be more naming and less strenuous diplomacy involved in the job, it would have been perfect.

Calum engaged his translator implant and listened in to the discussions still going on in the kitchen. Not surprisingly, the

Peloquin pair were trying every trick in the book to get an audience with him, but the liaison Sneijder had left behind did a fine job of stonewalling. Eventually it was his mother who brought peace to the house by turfing them all out.

A quiet knock on the bedroom door.

"Can I come in?" It reminded him of when he was a teenager, made him smile.

"Of course," he said.

His mother sat on the end of the bed. "Is it always like this in your job?"

He nodded, shrugged. "Can be," he said. "Cultural imperialism is a big deal. There's a lot of prestige awarded when one race's languages are used for naming over another and it can all get a bit heated. There have been wars fought over the naming of a new planet, civilisations wiped out. In fact it's one of the reasons the Bloc exists. It was originally set up to ensure fairness, and encourage harmony and trade, but in lieu of conflict the various races have developed internecine oneupmanship to a fine art. My job is to ensure that all of the languages in the Lexicon are represented equally while at the same time apportioning a name that is apt."

"Sounds like a bit of a juggling act," his mother said.

"Mostly, it's close to impossible," he replied. "There's so much diplomatic bartering involved that your newly discovered planetary system ends up with a nomenclature comprising a hundred different languages. It's a mess."

"How do you decide which languages to use then?"

"We cross reference terrain, flora, fauna, weather types – a whole bunch of criteria – and derive the names from the things that we already have names for. The Lexicon provides a ballpark and we go with that. The races whose languages are used gain a little extra cultural clout in the world in question." He sighed. "Which is why discovering a plant on Earth that resembles a species we have just named using a Peloquin language is a problem."

"Why?"

"If we use the same nomenclature, it gives them the first non-human cultural claim on Earth."

"That doesn't seem very fair. They don't let people name the plants that are grown in their own gardens?"

"Existing species are fine, they've already got names. And if contact had been yesterday, before we were adopted into the Bloc, we could have used any language we liked to name this thing. But on a Bloc world any newly discovered species has to be named using the Lexicon. And all of Earth's living languages – English, Mandarin, Spanish, German, all the way down to Gaelic and Swahili, everything that's taught in schools – are in the Lexicon. And they *know this*."

His mother looked shocked. "You think all of this is deliberate?" She whispered it as if she might be overheard.

"I'd bet on it," Calum muttered. "Of course we can't prove that I didn't bring back some germ with me from Ghessareen. That whole operation was such a mess that I'm not even certain of that myself. I'd be surprised if they don't conveniently provide a very clear trail of evidence to prove it. So I'm afraid they've succeeded. There's nothing we can do."

*

It was lunchtime when the call came through. Sneijder, who had smartened himself up in the intervening time, was back on the orbital. Calum recognised a canteen that had been turned into a makeshift hearing chamber. The Bloc representatives could be seen assembled in the background of the picture.

Calum had set his phone up to take in both his and his mother's deckchairs and the susurrating rust-silver tree that now overhung the corner of the garden.

"Calum, you've had time to consult the Lexicon. The representatives are eager to hear your judgement," Sneijder said. He fidgeted. "I should advise you that this call is being broadcast to the United Nations." He looked like he wanted to say more, but in the end didn't. The fact that Calum hadn't heard from Sneijder before this just meant that their hands were tied diplomatically as surely as they had been euonymically.

Calum straightened himself in his chair. "Yes, indeed," he said. He had spent the last few hours trawling all of the languages in the Lexicon for an alternative. Sneijder's silence confirmed what he already knew. That there was none. There was a clear path of semblance and antecedence. No matter what tack he took the Lexicon always brought him round to using the Peloquin naming.

Calum looked squarely into the phone's little screen. The human contingent looked nervous, the Peloquin looked eager – but then they always did. He had delivered naming judgements to similar groups many times, and while some of those occasions had been fraught with complicated layers of vested interests, he had never felt so personally responsible before. That was the moment that he decided that he'd had enough. He'd perform this one last naming and later he'd call Sneijder and resign. The job had so little to do with an ability with names that there had been little or no satisfaction in it for him for years.

"Oh aye, that's it is it? Loonging aboot, ye docksie pair, when I'm after my twaloors. What's all this oancairy onywey?" Aunt Bella's timing could not have been better. Calum's mum sprang to her feet to turn the old woman around and fix her something to eat in the kitchen, but Bella had already covered the ground between them.

"Calum, who is that woman?" It was Sneijder's voice, but the phone's screen was blocked by Bella's stout frame. "I can't make out a word she is saying."

"Aye, well?" Bella said, either ignoring or not hearing Sneijder. "Brian, son, you look awfy peelie-wallie. You maun be scunnered with all the palaiver that's been ongaun the day."

Calum looked at Bella with wonder. That was the word. *Scunnered.*

"Calum?"

That was the euonym for the feeling he had been trying to name since Ghessareen. Scunnered. In fact, *pure scunnered.* He'd not heard that word in years. Like most Scots words, it was essentially dead in linguistic terms. The old language, a historical victim of wave after wave of cultural erosion, had been steadily supplanted over generations with Anglicisms, Americanisms, Euroisms and most recently the backwash of intergalactic contact. Only the eldest in the rural areas still used it, spoke it, thought in it. Calum had been steeped in the Lexicon so long he had almost forgotten it existed. A few of the words had been absorbed into English, but never having been ratified as an official language in its own right, the Scots tongue hadn't made it into the Lexicon.

"Calum, if you can sort out the domestic business as soon as possible." Sneijder didn't try to hide the sarcasm. "The representatives are waiting."

Calum reached around Bella, spoke to the screen. "I'll call you right back." Then he took his elderly relative by the hand and led her gently to the knife tree.

"Bella, how long have you lived around here?" he asked.

"All my puff," she replied, looked at him sidelong. "How?"

Calum grinned. "I think you just might be about to save the planet," he said. "See this here? We're having a lot of trouble with it." He indicated the tree. "What would you call it?" *In your native language, that's not in the Lexicon.*

She peered at the plant: examined it slowly from its impenetrable roots right up to its branches and the deadly hanging blades of its leaves; twanged a steely twig with her finger. "Aye it's a scunner for sure," she declared at length. "You should howk it out and chuck it on the midden."

"A scunner, is it?" he asked, seeking confirmation.

"Aye, a scunner right enough." That said, Bella turned to Calum's mother. "Now, Magret, I'm hauf stairved, here."

35

Neil Williamson

"A *scunner* it is then," Calum said to himself, and picked up the phone. They weren't going to be happy about the use of a local language not in the Lexicon. In fact they'd be arguing about the legality of it for years. And by the time they sorted it out it'd be someone else's problem.

Now he'd made the decision he knew it was the right one. And now the feeling was gone, he was aware that it'd been with him for a lot longer than he'd realised. Before coming home, before Ghessareen even. A long time...

Scunnered.

He knew there had been a word for it.

The Bone Farmer

"Where are we going, Daddy?"

David could not look at her. Her eyes were water-blue, brimming with questions. He concentrated on starting the car while he searched for an answer that was not a lie, and he jumped when the wipers came on, sweeping away a season's dead leaves. Weak November sunlight washed the interior, highlighting the pallor of her face. Her skin had taken on that stretched translucency, a blue vein pulsing gently, snaking up under her thin blond hair. Sophie buckled her seat belt as he had shown her. She did this slowly, as if her hands inside her mittens were painful, and then looked up at him expectantly.

David was conscious of the urge to hug her to him, this fragile splinter of a child wrapped in coats and blankets on the seat beside him, but his fear of her condition overwhelmed it.

Instead he forced the rusty gear shift into first, released the handbrake and eased the vehicle out into the street. In his rear view mirror Anne McGivern was standing, arms folded around an old 12-gauge, grasping it tightly to her body against the cold wind and the failure of his resolve. Her eyes were hard with determination, masking the sorrow he knew she felt. She was still standing like that, as if frozen, when the car crested the hill on the north road out of town and he lost sight of her.

Sophie asked again, "Where are we going?" This time an edge of anxiety to her voice. "Is Mum coming too?"

Lisa had not come. It was better this way.

"No sweetheart, Mum's not coming. It's just you and me." His voice sounded strange, thin and hard; brittle as ice, brittle as his daughter's life.

*

Grey fields stretched either side of the road, hard earth neglected for so long, turned to scrub. David drove slowly. The sun was low, sullen; its light baleful. He had to squint around the visor to see the road. Not that there was any danger from other traffic, of course, but he had not driven for some time. It was best to be careful.

Sophie was tired and her breathing deepened, becoming easier, less wheezy as she drifted into sleep. Her head, noticeably swollen, lolled on her shoulder. Listening to her he could almost believe that she was well, that they were both back safe in the arms of the community, back home with Lisa, and that this journey had never been necessary.

Sophie woke as they passed through what had once been a fairly large village. She doubled up in a fit of thin coughs. It was all he could do to resist the urge to comfort her, keep his hands on the wheel, keep driving. He was pretty sure the place was deserted but he was not going to stop and find out. Anyone left here would certainly try to kill them once they laid eyes on Sophie.

"There's a bottle of water on the floor by your feet,
sweetheart." He watched and almost felt the pain etched on her
face as she fumbled off her mittens and tried to manipulate the
bottle top with those rigid claws that used to be her fingers. She
managed to gulp a little down but most of it slopped out of her
mouth, overspill from her constricted oesophagus.

*

How long had it been? He counted back two weeks to the day
when Sophie had gone missing. He remembered spending the entire
night holding Lisa close, by turns comforting her and restraining
her from leaving the community to look for their child. Not that
the others would have let her of course. It was one of the first
rules. No one enters, no one leaves. *Stay away, stay awake.*

They had seemed impressed by his calmness, his composure.
It was relatively easy once Lisa had eventually succumbed to
sleep for him to slip unseen to the car pool. By the time they
heard the engine it was too late.

When he returned he got as far as the edge of town before
they stopped him. Four shotguns followed him as he slowly
climbed out of the car. He could see Lisa. She was weeping and
struggling to reach him and Sophie. Anne and Bobby were holding
her firmly by the arms.

He appealed to them. He had found Sophie less than a quarter
of a mile out of town, fast asleep in a farmhouse. There was no
danger, surely. She said she had seen something in the sky, followed
it and got lost. That's all. She had made no contact at all during
that time. He didn't tell them about the delicate doll he had found
cradled in the child's arms. A stylized figure carved from bone,
bleached white, light and insubstantial; a featherweight thing. He
had crushed it to powdered fragments under the heel of his boot
while she slept.

He watched as they conferred. Some were adamant, some
were swayed by pity. People he had thought were friends said no,

39

looked away. Others he barely got on with pleaded his case with passion, he guessed for the sake of the child. Eventually they were granted quarantine. Eight weeks. If the symptoms had not shown by then, they could rejoin the community. Eleven days later in his converted police cell they told him that Sophie had begun to complain of headaches and stiff joints. David did not cry then. The loss had been inside him since the night she had disappeared, the tears shed over a mess of bone fragments while his child slept on in her innocence.

In the next cell his daughter was waiting to die, a grotesque and agonized end when it came. He was grateful that she had not been told. Alone in his own cell he waited for the stiffness to creep over him as well; the cancer pervading his marrow, fusing his joints, squeezing the life out of him day by day. He knew it was coming. He had been waiting for it for twelve years.

*

They had moved out of the city early. He could not have stayed there any longer, waking up every morning certain he could feel it in his legs, in his lungs; then realising that he had been granted one more day's reprieve. Lisa had called him paranoid but she had assented all the same. That was just the first move of many. Each time they moved further north, they became more remote from the population. Lost contact. Towns were becoming more insular, more suspicious of strangers bringing the disease from the south. They had only been adopted into this community because Lisa was pregnant with Sophie by that time. Five years ago.

Having been accepted, they were told the rules. The community was completely self-sufficient in everything: food, water, fuel. There was no necessity for any of them ever to leave. If you did, you did not come back. The only exception was sometimes when someone died. Then volunteers took the body away in one of the cars to be buried a safe distance from the living. They accepted the risks, the enforced quarantine, because every life seemed significant now, precious. This way was more dignified and personal than a cremation; and besides, there were sometimes fragments left after a burning.

*

To begin with Lisa was there every day talking, crying, just sitting on the other side of the door, being there. She took turns between Sophie and David although she spent most of her time with the child. Sometimes Anne came with her. Anne was really the only person in the community they could call a close friend, especially this last year since Kim died.

During the days before Sophie started showing symptoms, Lisa spent less time with David. The times she did sit with him, were spent in mostly one-sided argument.

"There's nothing we can do, Lise. It's the rules."

"But there's obviously nothing wrong with you. You're both clear. They'd know by now if you weren't. Normal incubation period, seven days, right? Why don't you make them see that? How can you just sit there and not even try? How can you be so fucking passive?"

"Because I don't know I'm clear. I don't know Sophie is. Not for sure. I feel okay, but we have to wait it out. The full eight weeks. I can cope with that."

"Well how the hell do you think I feel? I just want you back."

*

David stopped the car at a fork in the road, trying to remember the direction to take. He had driven this road only once previously. It had been night then and they'd had directions. He remembered that journey in the dark. They had seemed to be heading downhill all the way before they reached their destination. He looked out at the contours of the countryside. To the left, the land swept down into a wide glen. David gunned the accelerator and eased the car in that direction.

"Daddy look!" Sophie's cry was sharp, so unexpected in the long silence that David reacted, stamping the brake pedal, bringing the car to an abrupt halt. He looked out of her window, following the line of her crooked finger pointing to the sky above the valley. At first he could not see whatever she had seen, but then it banked away from them and he caught sight of the triangular red sail scudding though the air. It banked full circle and then passed low over the valley floor, vibrant against the drab background. David knew that this was what Sophie had seen in the sky that day. From a distance she would not have seen the man dangling under the wing, would not have known it was dangerous. She could not know what a hanglider was.

"It's beautiful, isn't it Sophe?"

Sophie was entranced. They sat in silence watching as the hanglider banked again, a high arc. Then they lost it in the sun. Disappointment lined his daughter's face as she strained and stretched to find it again, but it was gone. She seemed to shrink back into herself, disappear into the blankets as David started the car once more, ready to move on. Then the hanglider was swooping low over the road. The red material rippled as the contraption turned exposing for a second the skeletal framework and the shape of a man hanging underneath, before it was arrowing away to the left back over the valley again and disappeared.

Sophie had seen the figure, a stranger, triggering the familiar children's litany. A whispered iteration, "Stay away. Stay awake. Not another soul to take."

*

After Sophie had first showed symptoms her health had deteriorated quickly. David had been able to hear her during the night. He had lain awake listening to the coughing and the laboured breathing, feeling frustrated by his isolation and guilty because

42

he was still clear. They were taking less care with him now. Actually coming into the room to deliver his food, staying and talking for longer than necessary. Treating him as if everything were all right. He hated them for it.

Sophie, on the other hand, was a definite risk. They were talking about how to proceed. They told him how much pain she would suffer in the weeks to come; how the illness would change her, deform her; how long she might have left. They told him that the food allocation would be tight enough this winter. Sophie could last as long as March. It would be kinder. It was one of their rules.

Lisa came the day after Sophie was diagnosed. He watched her through the tiny cell window. She looked terrible. Her face was drawn, eyes puffy red smears. She was nervous and distracted, only able to meet his gaze for seconds at a time. She paced back and forward and stammered when she spoke.

"You knew, didn't you? When you found her. You knew then and you didn't tell me."

He could only mumble apologies. It was true. He had known it was a real possibility, had resigned himself to it, to his own death as well. But he could have been wrong, couldn't he? Lisa had had so much hope. How could he have deprived her of that?

After that Lisa stopped coming. Anne came and told him that she was coping very badly with the situation. Her face was wet when she told him that Lisa had consented to let them end it for Sophie. David wept with her. It had been the same for Kim.

Two days later Anne arranged for David to escape into exile with his daughter. She had told Lisa, given her the opportunity to join them, but in the end it was just the two of them.

*

The sculpture was eight feet high. A pale human form, a dancer preparing to leap. It stood alone in the centre of an empty field, too far away to see in detail. It was made entirely of bone.

43

"It's like the dolly I found," said Sophie in awe.

David said nothing, but drove on.

More sculptures became visible as the road wound its way down toward the valley floor. Some were far in the distance, others loomed over the road so close that the definition of the carving was lost.

They rounded a corner on the hillside and David stopped the car. The valley floor spread out in front of them. A wide bowl split by the path of a lazy snaking river. Mostly it had been farmland, now gone wild. Here and there clusters of trees stood naked and exposed in the aftermath of autumn. David reckoned he could see for maybe a mile and a half down the valley. The road continued to wind its way among the hills on this side, ending in the distance at what looked to be a town of some size. They would not be going that far though.

The sculptures took his breath away. There were maybe a couple of hundred of them fanning out in all directions over the fields of the valley floor. A pallid delta sweeping down from a focal point which was hidden by the curve of the hillside, but which he knew lay somewhere along this road.

Sophie was also enraptured, even more so than she had been when they had seen the first of the statues. She gazed down over the scene, drinking it all in with wide eyes. David had hoped she would find it beautiful. Anne had suggested it. A place to be at the end.

The scene had the same impact on him the first time. It had been night then, the moon lending its own ghostly sheen to the parade of figures. There was a great stillness but also a strange potential of animation. He and Anne had sat for hours in silence, the scene bleeding the last of their courage away, robbing them of words and action. Eventually, moved by the slow shift of light heralding the dawn, they had lain Kim's body by the roadside. They should have taken him all the way but this spot had been close enough for him to be found.

David reached over into the back and opened up the bundle

Anne had hidden in the footwell. Food, not much: bread, cheese and the last of the autumn fruits. An envelope of folded paper containing what he guessed were painkillers, again not many. More blankets were wrapped around binoculars in a leather case, a small knife and a large polythene tub of drinking water. And last, a heavy thing wrapped in cloth. He hid this away under the seat. It would be loaded he knew. Just in case the pain was too much for her, or for him. Just in case he saw things their way after all.

David cut the fruit into small pieces, watching Sophie swallow painfully, and helped her drink some water. Then he opened the binocular case and set the focus for the middle distance. He showed Sophie how to look into them. She held them awkwardly, as if they were too heavy. David found himself able to smile at the wonder she expressed at seeing the bone giants up close. He sat back listening to her describing the shapes she saw, enjoying the sound of her voice, enjoying too the tranquillity of the place, and wondering how long they would have here.

*

A sharp rapping pierced layers of sleep, hauled him back to consciousness. Sophie screamed. A face, a man's, bearded, solemn and wild eyed was pressed up close to David's window. He jumped, slammed his hand down on the door lock, reached over and did the same on Sophie's side and drew his daughter to him. The man backed away hands held open in front of him. His expression remained intently serious.

Clinging to him, Sophie calmed down some. They sat like that watching the man who had moved back about fifteen feet. David noticed his mouth was moving like he was saying something. With caution he wound down the window a crack.

"How many days?"

"What?"

"How many days has she had it?"

Cautiously David answered, "Seventeen. What concern is it of yours?"

The bearded face looked pained.

"It might not be too late. Why don't you bring her down to my home and I'll see what I can do?"

"What do you mean?"

"I'll make her better," he said, taking a step towards them.

David barked a harsh disbelieving laugh.

"You can't be talking about a cure. That's sick. Get out of here and leave us alone."

The man did not move but his large frame sagged as if under some unseen weight.

"I shall see her when it's all over anyway, but it doesn't have to be that way." It finally dawned on David who this was. He felt a crawling uneasiness. They called him the Bone Farmer. No-one he knew had ever spoken to him, but everyone at the community knew him. It was the Bone Farmer that took care of the dead. They said he was crazy, dangerous. He didn't look dangerous. He looked lost, exhausted.

The man continued, "Look it's getting late. At the very least I can offer you food and warmth for the night. If you want you can leave and spend tomorrow alone together. And the next day, and the next. You'll have that long at least."

He was right, David knew. At least they would be able to save on supplies. But he still was not sure. Sophie began to shiver at his side.

"I don't know."

The big man sighed again.

"What have you got to lose?"

*

The Bone Farmer's place was about half a mile further down the road. The route had taken a sharp turn back into the hillside to navigate a gully. There was a bright stream hurrying down a channel through the scree. They crossed a sideless, single-width bridge. Coming out round the hill once more, the road passed a church, a brooding grey shape clinging to a rocky promontory which jutted out over the valley. The walls, dark and imposing, built of the stone which made up the hillside, made the church appear as if it had been grown rather than built. The leaded windows were high and narrow and the main double doors were solid wood; both of these reinforcing the impression that the church was a natural part of the hill. To one side there was a walled graveyard which sloped steeply away behind the building. The outline of a large tree loomed there, obscured from view by the spire.

The next corner took them back into the hill and sharply downwards. The village to which the church belonged appeared ahead of them, a thin line of buildings extending along both sides of the road. The house closest to them was a little apart from the rest, closer to the church, and was a little higher up the hill. Like the rest of them it was built of the same dark stone as the church, giving it an air of austerity, but this one at least showed signs of habitation.

At the man's instruction David stopped the car beside the manse and with Sophie in his arms he followed him into the building. The man showed him to an upstairs bedroom, cold and musty from disuse, and then left them alone. Sophie was worn out from the journey, and without protest allowed her father to lay her on the bed and wrap her under the duvet. The man reappeared with a glass containing a small quantity of a syrupy liquid and a mug of soup.

"Give her this first," he said, proffering the glass. "It's a sedative. And the soup will warm her. I'll be down in the kitchen."

Sophie's eyes, red and sore, were already half shut. David had to shake her gently to wake her so she might to drink from the glass he held to her lips. She made a face, but swallowed without protest. Sophie was asleep before David had managed even to offer her the soup. He tucked her in and went downstairs.

Neil Williamson

In the kitchen the Bone Farmer was standing at a black iron range stirring a large pot. A warm meaty smell mingled with wood smoke.

"Want some of this yourself?"

David nodded and sat at the table. The man brought over two bowls and they ate in silence. Finally there was room for conversation.

"Thanks," said David. "That was good."

The man just looked at him, grunted. That same intense expression on his face. "Where you from?"

David looked away, examining the surface of the table, the empty soup bowls, wondering how much it was safe to tell the stranger about their community. But he felt the need for suspicion draining out of him. He was tired, he wanted to trust someone.

"Village called Invergourlay. About twenty two miles south west of here on the other side of the ridge."

"I know it. You got many souls left there?"

"Twenty nine. Not counting Sophe and me."

Surprise lifted the heavy eyebrows. "That's quite a few. For round here. How's your harvest been this year?"

"Not as good as last year. None of us are farmers really, a lot is down to luck. We always find it hard this time of year."

The bearded head nodded slow agreement.

David asked him, "What about you? How do you manage?"

"I've got a few sheep, some chickens, a vegetable garden. I do all right."

"You're alone here then?"

"Yes." Simply put. Not, *Yes, everyone else moved on but I stayed behind*. The implication was that everyone who had lived here was dead.

Softly David asked, "Did you bury them all?"

The man was no longer looking at him and David could see the weariness showing at the corners of his eyes as if the stern mask had cracked around the edges.

"I bury everyone."

48

The Bone Farmer

"How come..." David stalled, aware he was delving too deeply into the man's sorrow. The Bone Farmer already knew the question, however.

"How come I'm not dead as well?" He looked up again at last and his gaze had lost its intensity, his eyes soft bruises. "Would you believe I'm immune?"

In response to David's reaction, the man's face stretched into a thin smile.

"Ironic isn't it? How isolated everyone has become. No-one talks to anyone else. They just struggle along on their own and send their dead to me. No-one takes chances with the sick. Sometimes they throw them out as soon as the headaches start, sometimes they shoot them on the spot. One of the outcasts found his own way here once, looking for somewhere to die. I shared my blood with him, and he stayed with me for a while."

David could hardly believe it. "You gave him an open transfusion?"

The man's expression remained implacable, "It worked, didn't it? Gavin lived here for six months."

"Shit." Unwelcome possibilities were blossoming in David's mind. "What happened then?"

The intensity was back in the man's eyes, his voice carried a raw edge.

"He went home to spread the good news. Within a week he was back, dumped at the side of the road. With a bullet hole in his head."

David felt outrage and amazement well up. "If you *are* immune there must be some way to make them listen. You can't just sit here feeling sorry for yourself, you have to keep trying."

The man's eyes flashed angrily for a second, but it faded quickly.

"Maybe you weren't on sentry duty the last time I tried to tell your town," he said wearily. He unbuttoned his shirt, opening it fully to show a livid scar which creased the left side of his lower abdomen. "I got this for my trouble. Wasn't the first time

49

I've been hit, but if I can help it, it sure as hell's going to be the last."

David could only shake his head. "No, look, I'm sorry. If we'd known..."

The man's laugh was short and harsh. "Story of my life. Believe me I still try, but what can I do? If I let myself get killed, what then?"

David sat silently absorbing all this. Finally, warily he said, "What about Sophie?"

The man spread his hands before him.

"I meant what I said. I can cure her. I'm no medical man, but I do know that incompatibility and the risk of blood poisoning alone should kill any chance of it working. But it does work, somehow. She is still young, still growing. The deformities in the bone won't disappear but they won't get any worse either. Probably she'll look better as she gets older. I don't know. I'm just guessing. Maybe she'll always move a bit stiffly, find her breathing difficult, but she's got a better chance than most at a decent life."

Quietly David said, "I still don't know. I'll have to think about it."

"Of course."

David got up and went outside. He was scared about the extent to which he was putting his trust in this stranger, wanting so badly to believe him. Deep in thought he made his way up the curving road towards the church. Evening was coming on, spilling shadows among the hills. The west facing wall of the church glowed in the deepening light like the inside of a kiln, the leaded windows shimmering warmly.

Approaching the church, he walked out onto the rocky promontory, bringing most of the valley into view. To the east, the town at the head of the valley was becoming harder to determine, painted out by a wash of twilight. He made his way down the path which led around the church towards the graveyard. He rounded the corner, and then stopped.

The graveyard was thirty yards to a side, surrounded by a crumbling two foot high dry stone wall. Because of the lie of the land it sloped steeply downhill and was bordered at its farthest boundary by what had once been a field. The plots were arranged in regular rows. Closest to the church the grave stones were ancient, worn smooth. More recent stones were further away, and at the very back, simple wooden crucifixes. The neat rows of crosses continued into the field below the stone wall, spreading out to the sides, curving around the hillside. There had to be at least two hundred plots but David could not see their full extent. They were obscured by the towering shape of the tree.

The tree seemed to have originated at the end of the original yard, but had long since outgrown it and had in places reduced sizeable portions of the boundary wall to rubble. Its colour on the whole was pale, yellowy white, tinted pink by the setting sun. Rather than a trunk as such, the main body appeared to be a collection of entwined boles which bifurcated and branched, reaching thirty feet at least into the air, and then split and split again into the slenderest of stems, sweeping down to the ground like a willow. The roots, a tortured white tangle, twisted and spilled into the earth all around it.

As he got closer, David could see that the roots reached out into the field beyond, and then it dawned on him what he was seeing. What he had taken for a tree was in fact an impossible growth of bone, seeded in the graves, rising through the hard earth, turning, shaping it seemed at random, fusing together into the semblance of a trunk and branches, and then splitting off and bending low to the earth again to be absorbed back into the body of the whole. Still closer he began to resolve the vast central mass into a more complex snarl of bizarre shapes: ridges, fans, curving plates and knobs jutting out at all angles.

In many places large sections had been hacked away only to be replaced by virgin material. Moving around the tree, David found a large band saw propped against it beside a fresh four foot by three foot gash. Reaching the wall, he saw that the tree

51

was straddling what was left of it. In truth, it seemed more that the mass of roots was in the process of absorbing the chiselled stonework.

From here David could see down into the valley. The field beyond contained more plots than he had at first thought, all linked to the tree by ribbons of white snaking through the soil. But his gaze was immediately drawn to the parade beyond. Seeing the figures much closer now than before David was awed by their variety and simplicity, their pale, motionless beauty. Each was a sketch in the simplest of lines shaped from a rough hunk of bone, the semblance of a figure in the act of one of a myriad human functions: a tennis player; a woman ironing; a child playing peek-a-boo; a straining figure struggling with an umbrella blown inside out; a lollipop lady holding up non-existent traffic; a man with his head cocked as if listening to something, perhaps a joke; an old woman curled up in a foetal position, arms crossed over her head; a couple, limbs and torsos entwined, indistinguishable in an act of love; a young man tearing his dreadlocks, screaming. A catalogue of human activity, row upon row of stances and postures stretching down the hillside and fanning out along the valley floor. They were too numerous to count, but there had to be at least as many as there were graves.

Those nearest, crowding the graves like funeral mourners, appeared to be less clear than the others. At first David assumed this was because they were the oldest ones and had succumbed to weathering. But further study revealed that they were losing definition not because material was being worn away but rather because it was still being deposited, overlaid, still growing. These were figures in metamorphosis, taking on a new form. Less and less human, more and more... the word which sprang to mind was *natural*.

David's eyes drank them in, flitting from one, lingering on the next. He felt a chill breeze against his cheek as he studied the Bone Farmer's work. Behind him the wind teased a hollow multi-timbral tune from the tree's thinnest branches. It was a natural sound. Not creepy, he thought, merely melancholic. As the breeze grew in strength, ruffling through his hair, David began to pick out a low wavering ostinato from somewhere within the crowd of figures, a sorrowful counterpoint to the tinkling song of the tree. He hugged himself for warmth as the wind tugged harder at his coat and trousers. More voices, elicited from white, porous mouths, joined the first. Soaring discords, swelling to become a choir, weaving complex, atonal fugues.

Why had he come here? For Sophie, he told himself; but also, he realised, for selfish reasons. He had waited all these years to be taken by the plague, listening nervously with his body for sounds of growth within him. He had accepted the inevitability long ago, but it had never come. It had destroyed his daughter instead. At that moment he would have given anything to take her place in this field. All that was left was to stay with her until the end and then maybe linger a while and watch what her bones became in the hands of the sculptor. He owed her that at least. Remotely David felt as if he should feel repulsed at that idea, but standing here, watching and listening, there was a rightness to it, as if it was the most natural thing in the world. And it made it easy to try and ignore the painful splinter of hope that had lodged in him. But there was hope wasn't there? If the Bone Farmer was telling the truth. But how could you believe a man who spent all his time in this desperate place. How could anyone stay sane here?

He hugged himself harder, feeling raw emotion welling up inside him. He wanted to sing too, to join in. He thought about Sophe and Lise as they had been only weeks ago and he wanted to cry. He thought about everyone else he knew, had ever known, had met years ago in a swing park, at a cinema, on a trip to the seaside during one of those sticky hot August weeks only remembered from childhood. The wave reached his throat and broke, coming out finally a gasping half-sob. David rubbed his damp eyes with the heels of his hands, turned and walked back to the manse.

Neil Williamson

He had not realised how dark it had become and, approaching
the house from above, he saw for the first time that there was a
conservatory round the back in which lights were burning. As he
neared he could see the figure of the man inside. He was working
around a new block of bone, chipping and sanding, forming and
smoothing, although the final design was at this stage impossible
to guess. David watched as he walked toward the back door and
did not see the tarpaulin until he tripped over it. Picking himself
up he saw that he had stumbled over the hanglider: the tubular
framework around a small petrol motor and the red sail folded
away under the waterproof wrap. He found the back door and
went in.

In the conservatory the man was smoothing the top of the
chunk into the shape of a head. Without looking up, he said, "I
once took the glider down as far as the city. Only once, mind.
Once was more than enough."

David's face was tight, and when he spoke it was in a small,
hot voice, "She followed you that day. It's your fault."

The man continued as if he had not heard, "You know what
the city was like, David? It was the worst thing. A whole new
architecture."

"She found a doll, a sculpture. One of yours. It's all because
of you."

The man straightened and turned to face him, his chisel
forgotten in his hand. His features were rigid with suppressed
pain.

"How do you think I feel, knowing that? I made that doll
when I was laid up with a shotgun wound. How was I to know a
child would find it?" He suddenly whipped his arm around and
slashed the chisel across the unformed head. "I do all I can,
because only *I* can. I bury the dead and at the same time try to let
people know it doesn't have to be this way. And I make the
witnesses. Every death, a new witness."

The man took a step forward, seizing David by the shoulders,
forcing his face up close so that David could see the true wildness

54

in his eyes. "Did you see the witnesses? Did you hear their song? Do you know what it means? It means that it's all over. God has given up on us." His grip tightened, "But I still have to try, don't I? I still have to let them know I can save them all. I still have to give my blood to the sick. They do get better, you'll see."

David found the strength to throw the man off, barked, "Just leave Sophie alone you crazy bastard."

The man took a step backward, looking genuinely surprised. "But how can you not want... I mean, I already did. When you were outside."

*

A perfect full moon picked out the car at the side of the road looking down into the valley. Sophie was asleep again. David listened to her breathing as he gazed down along the valley floor. It could almost have been the sound of any child asleep. He knew he would have to start the car and move on soon, before she woke, but he did not know where they could go. Moonlight reflected brightly off the figures. From this distance he could almost believe the parade of witnesses was alive, marching down the valley.

Captured, watching the statues, listening to his daughter's life, an effortless constant, in and out. Listening real hard he was sure that Sophie's breath was lighter, less constricted tonight. Or perhaps he was just hearing the wind bearing a distant song.

The Happy Gang

Hello there, Doctor, I see you have found me at last. Here in my refuge. I'm able to walk further every day, but I suppose I should have known there is no outrunning you and your forms. Isn't this a beautiful corner of the village? So peaceful? No?

No, I can see you have more insistent priorities this afternoon than the simple pleasures of an apple orchard.

You want me to tell it again, don't you? You want me to change my story, give you something you can put in a report. You want me to say it didn't happen. To be honest there are times when I'm not even sure myself any more. That's what you want to hear, isn't it? That's your ticket to send me back. My return to sanity, my admission that I'm scared to go back.

Well, I am. I'm terrified.

That's how I know *he's* dead. The Captain.

But what does any of this matter. Crazy or sane, it's immaterial, isn't it? If I can walk and carry a gun your report will be signed and stamped, and I'll be sent back regardless.

Very well, Doctor. I'll tell it again, but it'll cost you a couple of your wonderful pills. You know I'm convinced they are a weaker dose. I can feel the shakes beginning and it has barely been two hours since my breakfast dose. Let me know if I miss out any of your favourite parts.

*

You know how I came to be in France, of course. I had been in the thick of it since the spring of 1916, serving at the front line as an MO with the 3rd Lancs. Then my father got wind of what was about to happen that summer, and he pulled strings, first getting me transferred to a field hospital behind the lines, then removing me further from danger with my attachment to the Surgeon General at GHQ. He would have had me back home completely if he could, but even Lord Hawthorne couldn't manage that. Still I suppose he did his best to keep me out of it, and having seen what I have seen it is no cowardice for me to say that I am thankful. 1916 was close to being the single most frightening time of my life. Close, but not quite.

By March of this year, it was obvious that the campaign along the Somme was going badly. Christmas had come and gone, and both sides had dug in for the long haul. GHQ decided a morale boosting tour of the trenches was in order. The party was to be fronted by General Atkinson. They could hardly have chosen a less sympathetic man for the job. I was co-opted as an adjutant but my main function was to report back to the Surgeon General's office on the status of our medical facilities.

On the morning of the seventeenth of March 1917 we drove down from Amiens. Our first stop was the casualty clearing station at Albert. A school house turned into a miniature hell. The officers presented their usual bluff encouragement, but I could tell that one or two of our small party were shaken by what they saw. Every bed was full, and the spaces between the beds were occupied by pallets on the floor. Every one of those was full as well. There were bodies everywhere. Men awaiting surgery to save, or more likely remove, recently blasted limbs, plug body cavity wounds, patch broken heads, before being loaded onto the hospital train to Amiens or Paris. For some, surgery had not come quickly enough, their wounds bulbous with stinking, gangrenous blisters.

I had to hand it to those boys. They did a fine job of keeping a respectful silence. Only muted whimpers bore evidence of their suffering, and there was not a glimmer of disrespect for their superiors. The men who had led them to this. If the trench newspapers were to be believed, there was an attitude of derision spreading through our lines faster than lice, but there was no evidence of it here. Instead there were salutes and hand shakes, brave smiles, the occasional cheerful joke. Good lads all of them.

As we left the hospital we passed a young corporal sitting in the shade of the building, his knees up to his chest, arms folded around them. When he showed no sign of acknowledging our party there was a moment of awkwardness during which the officers bristled uncertainly, caught between the omission of the customary show of respect and the fact that there was obviously something amiss with the man.

"What's this fellow's trouble?" growled General Atkinson, eyeing suspiciously the soldier, who had started to rock gently to and fro.

"Shell shock, sir," advised the medic assigned to us for the visit. "It's unlikely he's even aware of your presence."

"Shell shock," Atkinson repeated as if trying the phrase out for the first time. It was still a new term then – it came with the new style of warfare, the big guns – although I've heard it used often since. You are fond of it yourself, Doctor.

Atkinson's face pursed sourly, as if the words tasted to him of cowardice. One good look into the soldier's eyes could have told him it was no such thing – they were focussed elsewhere entirely. A place from where there was little likelihood of return.

It is not a place *I* have seen, Doctor. Your theories are wrong.

I don't know how, but somehow my nerves remain intact. As I've told you, what happened to me was far crueler.

Our tour took us from Albert to the trenches themselves. At every port of call we were struck by the men's marvellous determination to prevail no matter what. You could almost have taken these soldiers for regulars, instead of the barely trained bunch of conscripts that they were: bankers, butchers and brewers, men my father's age standing alongside youths yet to have their first shave, clusters of school friends, entire sports societies transplanted from their Oxbridge clubs. All of them ice-numbed, glass-eyed and a world away from their former lives; the military rigidity and that thin veneer of darkly cheerful stoicism, all that kept them waking sane every morning. The officers contented themselves with that veneer but I knew better. I had been, albeit briefly before my fortunate reposting, where these men were now.

Our tour was not limited solely to the British troops. On occasion we were greeted warmly by the Canadians, and civilly by the embittered Anzacs. It became a routine, almost like a game: the General's bluff parried back by the troop's own with tight obedience and gritty humour. Then, at the umpteenth dug-out of the morning, a pit-propped hole in the ground housing a handful of men lined up stiff-at-attention for inspection, a boy stumbled down the stairs nursing a bloody hand. Looking back, I have recognised this as one of those moments when the tide of events meets the current of your life at the exact point of maximum interference, and the turbulence throws you off course entirely. If we had left five minutes earlier, I would have been back in the car with the rest of them when the shelling started.

As it was, this white-faced boy's arrival was to blow my life apart as violently as any shell. He stood dripping blood onto the lowest wooden step, caught between his distress and the awareness that he had interrupted a senior officer. The General and the rest of us stared back at him.

"One of your men, Sergeant?" Atkinson asked.

"Private Willis, Sir. Currently on sentry duty," the little Geordie sergeant replied sourly.

"Better get a replacement up there, then. We can't drop our vigilance for a moment, now can we?" Atkinson said this without taking his eyes off the lad. The boy looked as if he might faint.

"Yes, Sir," the sergeant said, and with a jilt of his head spurred one of the others into motion up the stairs. Willis had to come fully into the dug-out to let him pass.

"That's a clumsy wound you have there, boy." The way Atkinson said *clumsy* was as if to say that he found difficulty in imagining that anyone could be so ham fisted. "How'd you come by it?" he asked.

"A piece of shell casing, Sir," Willis whimpered. "It was hidden in the mud."

The General mused for a moment. Then he said, "Still," and there was a sharpness in that word like the unsheathing of his regimental sword. It sliced the air between them with military unequivocation. "Still," he repeated himself, "a trip to the field hospital's probably in order, don't you think? A short rest up there and you'll be as right as rain. I expect, eh?"

Willis nodded uncertainly, puzzled by the officer's tone but exhibiting too obvious relief at his words. The sergeant reacted quickly. "Lambert," he addressed another of his men, "Make sure Willis gets to the field hospital…"

"No need, Sergeant," Atkinson cut in. "Hawthorne here has all the necessary skills." I swear that was the first time during that entire trip he had as much as acknowledged my presence – and now it was to make me complicit in his tormenting of this young soldier.

Nevertheless, I deferred to his rank with a muted, "Sir," and looked at the wound.

Having had his fun, Atkinson decided that the tour was at an end. "Finish up quickly and join us back at the car," he said to me.

Suturing the boy's hand took longer than I'd first anticipated. The wound was not only deep but he had torn the webbing between the second and third fingers. To his credit, he made not a sound

61

the whole time, except to say, "I never did it on purpose, Sir."

"Of course you didn't," I reassured, quietly noncommittal, although I couldn't blame him if he had. By the looks of him he was pretty well scared enough to do something that drastic. As I finished off the stitches I wondered privately how long it would be before he turned up at the field hospital with a bullet in the foot.

What do I remember of those moments immediately after leaving that dug-out? I remember pausing for a second, trying to recall which direction to go. I remember a stickling of fine rain on my brow, a sudden and out of place, fresh meadowy smell, and a far away sound – a sound that did not become louder as such, but rather became increasingly *present* in my world. Then the detonation: a chaos of sound, and a heavy rain of stinking wet earth that thudded down on top of my suddenly prone body. My first thought was of Willis and his comrades and, shamefully, how fortunate I had been to escape their fate of interment in the caved-in dug-out. Perhaps, however, there might be some hope if I could locate the spot where the entrance had been and dig quickly, but even as I regained my footing, a second shell exploded and sent me scurrying in the opposite direction, all thoughts of Willis and his comrades blasted away.

I zigzagged haphazardly along the supply trenches between the lines as the earth flew into the sky and choking smoke billowed around me. I searched desperately for shelter, but nothing made sense to my eyes. Then I was almost tumbling down a set of dug-out stairs before I was aware that the entrance was there.

I stumbled down the stairs, confused and sickened, but what stopped me was the warm murmur of conversation – the intimate sounds of fireside company. So normal and welcoming a thing here amid the mud and smoke with the artillery pounding iron fists into the earth.

I descended cautiously, intrigued, and saw half a dozen soldiers in various poses of relaxation, apparently untroubled by the hellish re-landscaping undertaken by the bosche shells only a few feet above them. Three of them clustered, laughing, around a letter. The central figure of the trio seemed somewhat embarrassed by what was written there, but apparently did not mind too much. A lover's letter, perhaps? On the bunk above them another stretched out lazily, reading a tatty book. Two more sat around a small table, playing cards. Barring the uniforms the scene could have been from a holiday chalet on a rainy afternoon in Skegness.

Outside a shell hit close by. The lamps swung wildly, little falls of dirt pattering from the ceiling. My heart clenched.

"Wooh! Getting a bit stormy," the men chorused, laughing again. The shock wave kicked me down the remaining steps.

"Oh, hello!" One of the card players, a gangly young man with a flopping blonde fringe rose from his game. He peered in my direction, and then reached up to stop the swinging lamp. "That's better," he grinned, "we can see you now. Name's Marten," he said, extending a hand. His handshake was firm and friendly. "Well, come in, please," he said. "Would you like some tea? There's a pot on. Should be just about ready. Right, Gordon?"

His gaming opponent pulled a battered timepiece from a tunic pocket. "To a tee," he said with a nod of satisfaction. Gordon was an older, tougher looking man. There was a rough burr to his voice that made me look instinctively at his insignia.

"Cameronians?" I asked.

"Spot on," Marten answered. His own accent was similar to my own, a teased-out product of the public school system, but there was possibly a hint of a Scottish lilt there now I was listening for it.

I was offered a bunk to sit on, which I did gratefully, and a hot enamel mug was pressed into my hands. I had not realised until that moment that I was trembling.

"So, what brings you round this neck of the woods in weather like this?" Marten said.

They listened politely while I introduced myself and told them what had happened to me that day. Afterwards, Marten introduced the lads, referring to them collectively as The Happy Gang – although he did not bother to explain the nickname. My trembling subsided as I began to enjoy the comfort of the dug-out's camaraderie. I found myself liking Marten's quick wit and infectious humour. However, when I mentioned General Atkinson's name there was a chorus of hoots and boos. While I knew the command was becoming increasingly unpopular with the rank and file, I was shocked by such open derision.

"Atkinson's not a favourite around here I take it?" I ventured.

Marten chuckled. "The man's a baboon. An ape, I tell you, and with no more military sense. His only *strategy* is to hold the line, keeping us sitting here, waiting to be blown to little bits. Men's lives are cheaper to him than artillery shells. He goes through them fast enough." There should have been rancour in Marten's tone as he said this, but he spoke as if he were discussing a disappointing cricket result. The other men murmured their agreement.

It was then, as I looked round them, that I realised there was no higher ranking officer in the dug-out than my own. "Who's your CO?" I asked.

"Captain Braithwaite," Marten replied blythely.

"Where is he?"

"He's out picking flowers," Marten said, barely suppressing a smirk.

"Are you trying to tell me that your CO is a casualty?" I found the euphemism, not to mention his attitude, suddenly more than a little distasteful. If this Braithwaite had bought it, the humour of his men was callous in the extreme.

"No, Sir." Marten made reference to my rank for the first time. He had the good sense too to moderate his tone somewhat. "Captain Braithwaite is out picking flowers. He thought they would brighten up the dug-out a bit."

"In the middle of *that*?" Incredulity raised my voice, but it was then that I realised that the shelling was over.

Nevertheless, Marten let the opportunity to smart-alec me pass. "Cap's a very brave man," he said. "He'd do anything for us. Every man here owes him his sanity, if not his life." Again a chorus of enthusiastic assent from the other soldiers. The sense of fun was gone though. And I could not escape the feeling that I was missing something. While I could not believe anyone would go outside for such a frivolous purpose during an artillery attack, the man was clearly not present in the dug-out.

"Well, it's been nice Corporal Hawthorne," Marten said, "but it might be a good idea to take advantage of this break in the weather and see if you can get back to your General. Sutherland, here, will point you in the right direction." A stocky chap with a child's chubby cheeks jumped to his feet energetically and retrieved his helmet from the bedpost before waggling his eyebrows at me. The welcoming atmosphere felt somewhat tainted following the bizarre exchange concerning their Captain, but I still didn't want to leave – especially having heard so little about this extraordinary Braithwaite. And yet, I knew Marten was right. If there was a time to head back, now was it.

While Sutherland bounded up the steps ahead of me I turned to the assembled men. "I'd like to come back and meet your Captain Braithwaite some day," I said.

"I know he'd be delighted to make your acquaintance, Sir." Marten nodded agreeably. "Well, safe journey…"

An explosion right at the dug-out entrance sent Sutherland tumbling down the steps to land at my feet in a spray of debris. A second round of artillery exchange was under way. Sutherland, breathing hard, blinked in shock for a moment – I could see his brain processing what had happened.

At the same time as he said, "Stormy again. Probably need an umbrella," I heard a subdued, but distinctly terrified, moan. Added to my unexpected plunge back into the trench hell I thought I had left forever the previous year, that sound was enough to unnerve me to the edge of panic. By some instilled reflex I had drawn my service revolver.

"What was that?" As I said it, I stepped towards Marten.

The nerveless bastard looked straight back at me without blinking. "What was what?" he said.

My gaze flitted around the room. The rest of the men watched with interest, some with evident amusement. It wasn't right. "I heard someone," I said.

"Sutherland?" Marten shrugged his eyebrows laconically.

"Not Sutherland," I snapped. "Tell me again, where is your Captain?"

"I told you, Sir. He's out…"

"I don't believe you."

He stared back impassively, as if he didn't know what all the fuss was about.

"Marten," I said, maddened that he continued to deny the sound I had clearly heard, and desperate to make some sense of the situation. "I have reason to believe that something has happened to your CO. Understand that I will use this gun if you do not tell me the truth." I hardly knew what I was saying. It was a ridiculous threat. I had never shot anyone face to face, and I was pretty sure I did not possess the unwarranted ruthlessness to carry out my threat now. And it looked like Marten knew it. "Aren't you afraid?" I punctuated my words by rolling back the hammer of the gun.

The supercilious smile that came as he said, "Not a bit, Sir," almost tipped me into unreason. I would have done almost anything at that moment to wipe it off his face. I felt my finger begin to squeeze the trigger. Saw that he observed that twitch.

Another muffled sound. This time more of a scream than a moan. It came from the shadowy rear of the room. I strode over there, and discovered a curtained off alcove behind one of the empty bunks. I yanked aside the grimy cloth and found a man lying in a rough hollowed-out bed-shelf padded with blankets. He might even have been fairly comfortable were it not for his bound limbs and the roll of old bandages stuffed into his mouth. I had no doubt that this was the mysterious Braithwaite, but I could not for the life of me fathom what their purpose was in keeping him like this. Then I looked again. Something about the face, the soft jaw line, the straight sandy hair. *Braithwaite*. I had been at school with a Braithwaite. A cheerful chap with whom I'd passed many muddy, happy hours in the second fifteen.

Unbelievable that this could be the same person, but I could not doubt the similarities.

When I reached out, his eyes flew open, bulging wildly. I imagine I saw a flicker there that he recognised me too. Certainly, nothing else can explain what was to follow. As my fingers touched his shoulder, he trapped them between his wrist-bound hands. I struggled to free myself, but he held on with grim determination. When I looked back to the men for aid, I discovered the muzzle of Gordon's rifle six inches from my chest.

"I'm afraid we can't let the Captain go, Hawthorne," Marten said. "It's like I told you, my man. He's very, very good to us. So good that we have to keep him safe from any possible harm. We need him. It'd be our ruin, if he ever left us."

I had no idea what he was talking about, but the captive was clearly terrified, possibly to the point of mental breakdown. "Your Captain needs help," I managed, pain blooming in my hand as the man's grip tightened.

"Not possible," Marten shook his head. "No doctors for Braithwaite, I'm afraid. And that goes for you too. I'm sorry but you can't be making any reports about this. It's been difficult enough keeping him secret this long. Sorry, old man." Then he executed a what-can-I-do shrug.

Gordon levelled his gun at me and I knew then with absolute certainty that they were going to kill me. Perhaps in as little as a few seconds. My limbs were heavy, filled with the same icy water that beaded my brow, collected around my collar. I was aware only of the gun and of counting my hopeless breaths. And of Braithwaite's grip around my fingers, a hot, hot clench that tightened until I thought my knuckles would pop and dislocate, my slender finger bones splinter.

There was screaming, but it wasn't mine.

Braithwaite let go.

And I was no longer afraid. Of anything.

"I think it's time Corporal Hawthorne went for a stroll, Gordon," Marten said.

Everything after that was dreamlike, I remember it all vividly but none of it seems in any way real. I nodded meekly, accepting my fate and not minding. Allowed myself to be ushered to the stairs, even as the Captain began to wail again. As if he knew what was coming.

"Bye, then," I said, and began to climb the stairs, Gordon and his gun at my back.

Outside, on the firing step, peering into no-man's land, I noticed with surprise that night had fallen. A clear, black sky, prickled with uncountable stars, stretched across the blasted field. Bright wands of search light beams angling up from both sides made it feel like fairyland. That was what I thought of as I clambered out of the trench – that it was a place as ethereal as the music of Debussy. It utterly delighted me. I looked back once, saw Gordon watching from the shadows. He sketched a cheerful wave, and I smiled. It was a pleasant evening, and as I began to walk, I felt good. More than that. Happy. As if all my cares had been lifted from my shoulders. Even if I stumbled over the broken ground, had to pick my way between the blackened and shattered stumps of trees, all that remained of a once charming little wood. Even if I knew I was being watched with incredulity by snipers. Even if I was waiting for the bullets to come as soon as the Germans got over the surprise of this idiot Englander ambling along like a weekend promenader. Waiting for the bullets. Happy, I began to whistle as I walked.

The bullets came singing harmonics to my tune.

*

It's been two months since they shipped me back. I've healed well – you can hardly see the limp thanks to this Kentish weather and the country lanes that make my daily walks a pleasure. To all intents and purposes, I appear fit to return.

There. I've told it.

No, not quite all of it.

Because it's not really my health you're interested in, is it, *Doctor*? Not even my noted curious calm and good cheer while all around me here were jelly-headed wrecks. In fact, I even doubt that you are a real doctor – something about the way you mutter 'shell shock' as if it covers a multitude of mental malaises, the way our conversations loop around repeatedly to the nightmare I had three nights ago, the way you were unknown at this hospital until two days ago. The way you keep asking me, *how I know*. How I know details of the latest disastrous push along the Somme when the Commons haven't even been told yet. How I know, to the minute, *when* it happened.

What can I tell you? For two months I have lived without fear. Can you imagine that? No nightly terrors as memories of the trenches populated my dreams. In fact no dreams at all. No daily anxieties about being sent back, either. Going back would have been no more than a nuisance – after all I love it here. I possessed not one ounce of fear of death or danger. But not just that. All those minor trepidations that hamper one's life were gone too – fear of infirmity, fear of old age, fear of living a life unloved, fear of failure. All gone. I was confident, relaxed and generally happy with the world. If it was insanity it was a most benign form. I didn't even care what people would think of me for extenuating Braithwaite's plight by keeping quiet about it. I try to tell myself that anyone who witnessed the daily horrors of the Somme might have done the same.

Three nights ago I dreamt for the first time in two months. I dreamt of the trenches. We were crouched on the firing step, awaiting the signal. Then up and over the top, and immediately figures around me were spinning and crumpling amid a rattling hail of Maxim fire. One of them was Braithwaite. I woke screaming and sweating, and knotting my sheets in a heart-gripping panic.

I felt fear.

That's how I know what I dreamt was real.

And yes, now I'm scared of going back; and I'm equally

scared you won't believe this ridiculous story and report me as a spy. It has all returned after my cruel emotional lacuna, and it feels a dozen times worse than I remember. But at the same time, I know I've got it easy.

Think about this. Marten and his boys had a problem. It was all very well managing to keep the state of affairs under wraps in the long stretches of inactivity, but when the order came for that push, what were they to do with Braithwaite? If they left him behind they risked discovery, and faced court marshal, and much worse – losing him. If, miraculously, any of them survived. Really, they had no choice than to untie him, stick a tin hat on his head and a gun in his hand, and take him with them.

Good old Captain Braithwaite – a man who so cared about the young soldiers in his charge that he'd have done anything to help unburden them of their anxieties.

Imagine him as the whistles shrilled along the line, stumbling along behind his brave boys who strode ahead, shielding him as well as they could, unfazed by the notion of walking towards their deaths. Imagine the crushing weight on his soul of not only his own personal terror, the excess burden of six others.

I can't stop thinking about it, Doctor. Believe me, the foggy fields of shell shock would be welcome. Even death, a blessing.

But this war is neither generous nor even-handed with its blessings.

I wish I could tell you something that would have you certify me as unsuitable for service, keep me here until the war is over, but there have been enough lies. I thought of myself as a good man, but I have been colder and more callous than I would have believed capable of my nature. And all at the expense of a man who, even in his own terror, recognised me as one who once called him a friend.

Perhaps it is right, after all, for me to return to the front. If you have any compassion, Doctor, perhaps you would tell them that that is my wish. It is surely fitting for a man to choose to die in a place where he found happiness.

Cages

"Hello, Wilson. It's me, Jericho."

The old man's eye surveyed me blankly through the narrow crack; dull grey, blinking, once, twice, and then gone as the door closed again. My heart sank. I thought maybe he was having one of those days where he didn't recognise me, and I would have to endure the process of introducing myself, jogging his memory until he remembered. I called his name again and raised my hand to knock a second time, but stopped when I heard the tentative jangle and clack of the security chain being removed.

The door swung inwards at my touch. The tiny hallway was deserted. Old Wilson could move fast enough when he wanted. I hefted the grocery bags into the crook of my arm so I could close the door, and took them into the kitchenette.

"I got everything you wanted, but they only had plain flour and they'd run out of baking powder. Have you got any here?"

I paused putting the groceries away, waiting for an answer. It came eventually, indistinct.

"Doesn't matter."

I shrugged and returned my attention to the groceries.

"What is it you're making anyway? A cake or something?"

No answer, so I went through. I didn't see him right away, but then he turned his head slowly towards me and he was there in his armchair as always. The curtains were drawn, diffusing the light, leeching what little colour there was from the room. I ached to throw them wide open, but Wilson would complain like hell if I did. In the dim grey light it was hard to discern between his grey skin and his grey clothes and the threadbare grey fabric of the old armchair. As I passed the window I brushed the curtain, briefly allowing a hard bar of light to probe the room, touch his face, and he flinched as if struck. In that second of illumination I saw that he was crying.

He had been looking at the canary in the cage which sat in the corner. The bird's name was Buster. It looked dreadfully thin the first time I'd seen it, but at least it had most of its feathers and chirped occasionally. In the intervening weeks it had lost still more weight. Now it lay weakly on the bottom of the cage beside its water dish, on a carpet of its own feathers. It was not yet dead. I could see the rapid rise and fall of its delicate rib cage, the occasional blink of a helpless eye. In the two months I had been visiting Wilson I could not remember ever seeing him feed the bird. In the cage there was water, yes, but no food. I could well believe it was starving to death.

I don't think Wilson was a cruel man. Senile, forgetful to the point of neglect, perhaps. But not intentionally cruel. It was a desperately sad thing, but even so I found it hard to stomach.

"Oh, Wilson," I sighed, reaching a finger through the bars to stroke the bird. It was trembling. "Look at him. We need to get him to a vet." I looked back at the old man. He had not moved. "When did you last feed him?"

"Feed him?" His gaze travelled back to the cage. His voice was small, as if from a long distance. "I've run out of seed."

I made to reach for the handle of the cage, saying, "I don't suppose it matters. I'll take him away right now and get him some attention, okay? He'll be right as rain tomorrow."

"No!" The sheer unexpected volume of his voice stopped me. Like a crack of thunder from a cloudless blue sky, so out of place in this oppressively quiet room. Wilson was looking at me, his eyes incongruously bright, like new things set amid his faded paper features. He and I both knew there was no vet. Not for people like us.

The way he held my gaze froze me there until he spoke again. His voice returning to its normal pitch, held a note close to pleading.

"Don't take him, Jericho. Get the seed. It'll be alright if you get the seed. Just don't take him away. I need him here with me."

He got up and shuffled over to the sideboard where he rummaged around in a drawer for a minute or so. Eventually he emerged triumphant. In one hand he clutched a very crumpled piece of paper. He smoothed it out, before pressing it into my fist. There was an address written on it. A West End address, across the river. It would take me hours to walk up there and back.

"That's where to buy the seed."

"Wilson," I said as gently as I could, although in truth I was getting a little impatient with him. I could see little point. The bird was probably too weak to eat solids by now. Best just to let me take it away and put it out of its misery. "That's miles away. Buster might die before I get back."

He looked up at me levelly for a good thirty seconds, as if I were a slow student missing the point, before he said,

"I might die before you get back. But I don't want to. I haven't been out of this building for twelve years. Hardly even out of this room, out of this chair here. And I've always had my Buster. Lynn understood."

He pressed a thick wad of notes into my other hand. I protested.

"This is too much, surely,..." but he stopped me with a tired hand on my bare arm. His skin was cool and uncomfortably smooth; worn.

"Get my seed. Please." He sank back into his chair again. "I can't go. Even if I was fit, even if I wanted to, I couldn't. This room..." There was despair in his countenance now, and something else. He looked afraid. "I'm a prisoner here and I'll never, ever leave."

*

I took the stairs; eleven flights. The lifts hadn't worked for seven months and it didn't look like they'd ever be repaired. I wanted to believe I was just doing this to humour his senility, but part of me knew what he meant.

We are all confined by our circumstances. At least the *we* who live in these damp-ridden concrete towers, slowly sinking into the ever gluttonous Thames. Above the high tide mark and below the poverty line, sharing our homes with the rats and the roaches. Social Services' answer when you have no where else to go. Well, no one would live here from choice.

Lynn understood. She was his daughter. We became lovers soon after I came here; but more than that, I don't know, companions, *soulmates*. At least so I thought. We traded dreams attempting to raise our horizons beyond the concrete walls and the ever expanding mudflats. I never knew she had a father until she was gone, chasing her own private, desperate dream – the one I never shared – leaving a note which read, *Love you. Bye. Look after Dad.*

Prisoners of circumstance, yes; and Wilson even more so, physically and mentally bound to his tiny concrete cell of a flat. I think he may even have spent some time in jail, but I'm not sure. I visited him every three or four days, making sure he was alright, buying his food once a week. Every time I saw him it seemed he had faded a little more into the pattern of that room. That drab collection of featureless clutter. His life's possessions, all unremarkable individually, just an old person's *things* but together constituting a mosaic which had absorbed him. As if the pieces had subtly shifted around him over the years to make a place for him in the picture.

*

The seeds were expensive, costing almost all the money that Wilson had given me. I carried them home in a paper bag. He took the bag from me, carefully, almost reverentially, and set it down on the sideboard beside the cage. I hung back at the door. From there the canary inside seemed completely motionless. I wasn't sure it was still alive. He tipped the bag out onto the sideboard and began to sift through the pile of seeds.

"The man said it's mixed, I'm sorry. They didn't have just canary seed."

"Doesn't matter. There's bound to be some canary in amongst it. Ah." He had found what he was looking for. Wilson held several large oval-shaped seeds up to show me and then opened the door of the cage. Buster proved he was still with us by lifting his head a little to meet Wilson's hand. Then quickly, and so roughly I thought he must break its neck, Wilson forced open the bird's beak and jammed one of the seeds right down its gullet. The little eyes bulged as it choked the obstruction down and the bird collapsed again to the floor of the cage.

Wilson turned round, wiping his hands on his trousers and smiling broadly. Then he ushered me out, saying, "He's all right now. Come back tomorrow and you'll see him. He's all right."

*

Neil Williamson

It was a most beautiful thing. In that half lit room its feathers shone gold with a brilliance that bordered on luminosity as it flitted and darted around our heads. I couldn't help but laugh to see it, and to listen to the joyful music of its song. Wilson was chuckling quietly to himself and the happiness in his face gave me as much of a buzz as the miraculous bird itself.

And then I saw what lay on the floor of the cage. The joy drained out of me and I swear I almost threw up. I have said that I didn't think he was a cruel man, but even if he did not understand that birds must be fed more than the occasional biscuit crumbs, what else can you call his treatment of that poor creature. I gently lifted the wrecked carcass out of the cage and wrapped it in newspaper. The old man's attention remained fixed on the other bird which was singing away cheerfully on the top of the dresser. Buster. Sick joke, and it wasn't even intentional.

"How long will this one last, Wilson?" I said bitterly.

Again I was treated to that look of agonized patience.

"His life, my life. What's the difference? It's just a question of scale," he said.

I departed quickly leaving sour words behind me.

*

But Wilson was dying. We both knew it, and as much as I despised him, I could not leave him on his own at the end. The time came when there were no more canaries, and I refused to buy more of the seed. He tried other birds but only found joy in canaries, and once they were gone he faded quickly after that.

Near the end, he persuaded me to help him bake his cake. It turned out flat and solid, and we sweetened it with icing sugar and jam.

He said, "Let's have a picnic."

"Where?" I replied. "You're too weak to go anywhere, mate."

"On the roof."

I filled a thermos with tea, and packed it in a carrier bag

76

along with plates, cups, a knife, and our cake. I found one striped deckchair and a travelling rug, and carted them up five flights to the roof. After setting everything out near the west facing edge, I returned for Wilson.

"Are you a religious man, Jericho?"

I told him I wasn't. He said,

"I always wanted to believe in reincarnation, but I've never had faith. Not true faith, without question. I don't think many people have that any more. I want to believe that your soul goes somewhere else, but what if it just stays with the body? What if you just keep on going the way you were when you were alive?"

He died with a view across the city. It's all a question of scale. The birds came not long after. Slick newborn flopping onto the rug around his rent body. The wind soon dried them. I sat and watched, until dusk fell and it got cold. I could feel the currents of the skies pass around me, through me. The air was full of birds. I thought about what he said. And waited. Picking the seeds out of my teeth.

Amber Rain

When Colin raised the window to replenish the living room's baked air, he noticed the first specks of water on the pane. It was a fine rain, the kind that effervesces, prickles your skin. He watched the tiny droplets coalesce, gain enough mass to overcome the surface tension and stream down the glass. Each little river scintillated, distinctly pale amber in colour. An unnatural shade – even for Glasgow. Even in a time like now.

Of course, it was only a trick of the light. The city's atmosphere was never *that* toxic. Inevitably, after so many days of unrelenting heat, a foundry of cloud had massed over the city, compressing the evening's remaining sunlight to the weak radiance of cooling ingots. Soon those foundry walls would break open, flash-firing the city with summer lightning, and cooling its inhabitants with such a deluge that the pavements would steam.

Down in the street a woman was crossing the road. Colin only saw her for a moment before she darted between two vans, but there was something about her. Her hair was different, the style of her clothing – a strappy blue summer dress – unfamiliar, and it had been, what, eight months? He almost didn't recognise her, but he was sure that it was Paddy.

When the door entry rasped he almost ran to let her in.

Paddy was soaked through, and immediately headed to the bathroom to dry off. To give himself something to do, Colin slipped a few slices of cheese on toast under the grill. He remembered to be liberal with the Tabasco.

"Smells good," Paddy said, sitting at the table. She had found his old black jumper. It had always suited her, the way it framed the old Goth-chic cosmetic pallor she had favoured back then. She looked good in it now too – but in a different way. She'd allowed her hair to grow, washed out the wacky colours. Now it coiled loose around her face, strands clumped with some residual dampness she'd failed to towel out. Her face too – minus the habitual heavy application of eyeliner and the glittering encrustations of those once beloved piercings, she looked somehow both older and childish. At any rate, life appeared to be treating her well. The pallor gone, her skin radiated health. A sheen of perspiration anointed her brow, nose, cheeks.

"What?" she said.

Caught staring, Colin switched off the grill, and slipped the contents of the pan on to a plate which he placed in the centre of the table. "It's just a surprise to see you." He sat opposite her. "A nice one," he added, nudging the plate towards her.

She took a slice, chewed off a corner, trailing filaments of melted cheese. "Thanks, Col," she said at length, watching him pour two mugs of treacle-coloured tea.

"Thanks for what?" he said.

"I dunno – " she stalled, brow creasing as she searched for the right words. Steam from her mug rose into her face.

"I think I expected you to tell me where to go. But I should have known you wouldn't. You always were too nice by half." Paddy closed her eyes, inhaled the vapour. "It's so difficult now

– to know about people," she said, opened her eyes, offered a tiny smile. "Thanks for still being you."

Colin shrugged, returned the smile. As if still being himself was nothing, had required no effort to reconstitute his personality from the mess she'd left behind. As if *still being himself* could possibly have any kind of meaning. After five years with her, as a single entity – sharing a life, a home, a tight band of friends. Then four months of slick, almost invisible unravelling. One splintered evening of mutual abuse, the subject of which: an itemised mobile phone bill and one particular friend. Alan. Half an hour walking the streets to cool off, mentally drafting plans of conciliation. Then coming home to Life Without Paddy.

Colin was surprised to find that the anger he thought he had been saving up had somehow leaked away. He wasn't even interested any more in how the Paddy and Alan thing had panned out. There was no longer any resonance of the fury and frustration. In recent months, his flat had become a place he came back to only to sleep, or more often *not sleep*. It had been too long since anyone but himself had as much as spoken aloud in these rooms. He was just glad she was here.

"So, can I stay?" Her voice cracked.

"Reading my mind again?" An old shared joke.

"Yeah, and it's about as entertaining as that paper you work for," she rejoined. A spark of the Paddy he used to know. Funny how suddenly the flat felt a little like a home again.

The way it had felt when they were together.

Before the aliens came.

Colin watched television while Paddy took a bath. A political discussion show murmured away on turned-down volume. He was tired of hearing the protracted post-mortems caused by the Prime Minister's resignation the previous month. On one side it had become a blustering defence from the loyal elements within his own party – John MacDougall, they claimed, was ill, his unexpected resignation made under severe stress. At the same time, the opposition parties had launched into a feeding frenzy at the political opportunity, clamouring for a general election. Both sides continued to make nervous denials that, despite the recent claims of the country's erstwhile leader, the UK was *not* currently, nor indeed ever had been, host to agencies of extra terrestrial origin.

Colin flipped channels. Question Time was replaced by recent footage of the man himself. MacDougall looked haggard, spoke with uncharacteristic hesitancy, but Colin could see neither duplicity nor delusion in the man's face as he mouthed the words that had become his last sound bite.

"I'm sorry."

And, "No, I can't explain."

And, "There's nothing we can do."

Colin muted the television entirely, but the screen continued to sheet blue lightning around the room.

Eventually, back along the hall, the bathroom door opened. Colin waited a few minutes, switched off the set and followed Paddy through to the bedroom. She was lying on her side, facing away from the window, into darkness.

He lay down behind her. Not too close, but close enough to smell apple-scented bath-soak, and the dampness of her hair. He couldn't tell if she was asleep, but then she reached round and pulled his arm around her. He drifted off trying to listen to her breathing, but could hear only the rattle of rain against the window.

The only difference between Holyrood and Westminster was in the accents of the squabbling. The paper had sent Colin over to Edinburgh to photograph Hibernian's new French striker down at Easter Road. Afterwards, he'd taken the opportunity to drop in at the Scottish Parliament where the Education Minster was unveiling a new pay deal for teachers.

Colin watched from the gallery as the minister tried stoically to deliver her speech over the heckles of the Scottish Nationalists. He sighted her through the viewfinder of his SLR, focused the telephoto lens on the tension in her neck, around her eyes. A wayward strand of hair slipped across her face. He snapped her flicking it away.

"Does any of this *matter* any more?" A skinny, middle-aged man in denims farther along in the public gallery. He looked like he'd neither slept nor washed for days. The minister stammered to a halt, looking up at him, able to continue only when he had been removed by security. Colin framed a quick shot of the two uniforms huckling the guy away. That would fit nicely into the paper's *Out The Aliens* campaign – the most public face of a pressure group aimed at getting the government to back the ex-Prime Minister's story, and come clean about what was happening. A typically tabloid effort, but it was having an effect.

It didn't matter if MacDougall was lying, or mad, or, against all odds, actually telling the truth. Half the country believed him – half the world, it seemed, and many had also had, if not similar, then analogous experiences. Reports came in daily, everyone had a story, knew someone, who knew someone, whose husband, mother, next door neighbour had had an experience of some sort. *Aliens in My Watering Can, Aliens in The Television, Aliens in the Little Chef off the M74, My Grandfather is a Grey, My Teacher is a Pod Person, I was Seduced on Rohypnol by TV's Lieutenant Worf – and I was saving myself for Mr Spock.* The stories flooded in from Glasgow and Edinburgh, the remote reaches of the Highlands, all throughout Britain, Europe, the planet. From Finland to Portugal, Argentina to Canada, and oh, by God, yes, all over the States. Only, there was no evidence. No pictures. No recordings. Just stories. Few of the details were wholly consistent.

The media were loving it. Even if the world wasn't being visited, it was gripped by the *idea* of such an invasion. A quiet, nervous paralysis. Markets were down, investments delayed, everyone waiting. The politicians tried to keep things ticking along, but since they could neither officially prove nor disprove the stories it could only look like they were covering something up. The editors played the uncertainty like expert anglers.

Neil Williamson

When he returned to the flat it was so still that Colin assumed immediately that Paddy was gone. He had spent all day mulling over their strange, edgy encounter the previous evening, and had half convinced himself he'd dreamt the whole thing. He stooped to retrieve the mail from behind the door, placing the envelopes unopened on top of the pile of bills and circulars and invitations to take out new credit cards, and wondered what it took to upset things enough to bring society finally to a halt. If it was true that aliens were among them, how could it be that he could still buy fresh pesto in Safeway? How could any credit card company seriously offer him a free couple of grand and trust that he'd pay it back, plus interest? How did the buses run, and new movies open at the cinema? If the world was so overrun with extraterrestrials, surely it would all stop. And everyone would *know*. For sure. There would be photographs in the papers, amateur video footage, pictures of grey humanoids, shadowy space ships, *something*; interviews with astronomers, global summits, vigilantes, public unrest, martial law.

And because people would know, they'd recognise that they needed one another.

And Paddy would still be there.

For the second time in two days she surprised him. On the kitchen table Colin found two supermarket bags. Their contents: one bottle of Merlot, one packet of fresh cappelletti, one jar of pesto, mushrooms, capsicums, and a bag of salad leaves, with a bottle of Caesar dressing. Snap. His own bags contained the same – minus the dressing. Paddy had been a selective food lover. She knew what she liked, and if she liked it, she loved it. She'd hated Caesar dressing.

He found her in the bathroom. Colin hovered at the door, despite having seen her naked countless times before. From there he could see one leg arched above the rim of the bath. The leg glistened pale and pink under the stark bathroom light, and he could just make out part of what looked like a tattoo – a recent one, raw and scabbed – as the leg oscillated gently from side to side. The rhythmic lapping of water counterpointed their conversation.

"Thanks for getting the food in," Colin said. "And for remembering that I like that Caesar dressing. But you should have got something we both like."

"It's only food, Col. It doesn't matter to me. I don't have much of an appetite these days." Her voice sounded strange. Perhaps it was the acoustics that made it sound so distant. For a moment Colin wondered if she were on something. The thought was as absurd as the idea of Paddy having no appetite – she didn't even smoke. But then people changed, didn't they?

True to her word, when they had prepared the food, Paddy did little more than push it around her plate. Colin fared little better, the kitchen's humidity whittling his hunger to a vague discomfort. They made up for it, though, with the wine. They drank so they wouldn't have to talk, then took the second bottle into the bedroom to watch the now spectacularly torrential rain. It hissed onto the pavement outside, streamed down the drains, flared amber on the window glass as the streetlights stuttered to life.

Paddy turned away from the window, moved her palm from the pane to his face. Her hand was cool and clammy. There was something in her expression. Some kind of need. Colin remembered that she didn't articulate her feelings well, often needing help in finding the words.

"Paddy, what's this all about?" he began.

"Shh." She stopped his words with her fingers, and then as if they might leak through between them, with her lips, ensuring whatever he said was swallowed down inside her.

When they made love, skin to skin on white sheets rucked beneath them like time-frozen waves, Colin noticed that her skin was damp with sweat from the outset, and for the first time he wondered if she might be ill. Perhaps a flu virus of which she was unaware; maybe something more serious. The need he had sensed in her was obvious now in the hunger of her mouth, the

Neil Williamson

clutch of her hands on his back, the strength and urgency of her legs, pulling him deep into her, where she boiled around him with a scalding liquidity. It was as if her entire body were deliquescing from the inside out. And yet, even locked in her embrace, Colin felt external to the process. There had always been an element of this with Paddy. She was so contained. It was her way, when she allowed herself to be fucked, to keep her pleasures to herself, internalised. Eyes closed, focussing on whatever was going on inside her, acknowledging nothing else. When she came, her breath sounded like steam.

While Paddy slept immediately, twisted around with ropes of sheet, Colin found rest harder to come by. He was staring at the wedge of light fanning across her thigh, illuminating the tattoo. He could see now that it was a swallow – so unoriginal that it could have been picked at random from a tattoo parlour wall. The mundanity of it disappointed him. Outside he heard the occasional surf of cars passing along the rain-slicked street.

He was still awake when Paddy's sleeping body coiled itself tight and foetal and, shaking with tension, she uttered a sequence of throaty moans of such sexual intensity that he became immediately aroused, although he knew that her pleasure had nothing to do with him. Whatever caused Paddy such passion in her dreaming had more effect on her than he ever had. In a few minutes the shaking had subsided, her body relaxed, and the moans faded into the regular breathing of sleep.

*

It surprised Colin that Paddy persisted in hanging around. It was what he wanted, of course, but that he might get what he wanted did not seem right. She was waiting for him the next evening when he returned from a brass-monkey shift outside the Glasgow Sheriff Court where a prominent local mobster had been been convicted of several major drugs offences. Two frozen hours for a blanket-over-the-head shot at best.

86

Paddy was dressed for an evening out. Obviously she remembered that his Tuesday nights were habitually spent at the Carnarvon. This Tuesday Colin wasn't sure if he wanted to go, but Paddy persuaded him.

"It's good to keep these routines going, isn't it?" she said.

Colin didn't know what routines Paddy kept going. As far as he could tell she hadn't left his flat in two days.

The Carnarvon, a fair trek up to St Georges Road at the periphery of the West End, was all cigarette-burned leatherette and chipped Formica. They'd settled on it because the beer was cheap, there was no karaoke or covers band like the ear-splitting Young Neils, who 'rocked the free world' at the nearby Wintersgills at unpredictable intervals, and most of all because it had no more than a dozen other regulars. On Tuesdays they practically had the place to themselves.

That night, however, the pub was packed. They found Colin's friends crushed around a single table. Longer standing acquaintances raised eyebrows when they recognised Paddy. Colin looked around the assembly. Here were virtually all the people he might count as friends. A few: Dave, Archie, Ewan and Shell, were core Tuesday-nighters. Others were occasional attendees, partners or friends of friends. One or two faces he hadn't seen in years.

"The gang's all here," he said.

"Aye, and they're thirsty," replied Deepak, waving a half-full pint glass in his direction.

Glasses were filled and drained often during the evening, resulting in an unsteady megalith of towering glass on the table. Colin made the effort to keep the conversation varied, but inevitably it found its way back to the subject they were all trying to avoid. Ewan was forced to expend a deal of energy defending the numerous television science fiction series of which he was a fan. Their anthro-centric, American aliens, he argued, could not be expected to prepare the world for the *real thing*. It was only entertainment after all. Nevertheless, Dave said, the images these shows presented, along with certain block buster movies, formed the basis of public expectation when it came to the extraterrestrial, and *this* – what ever *this* was that was currently being experienced – was just too strange to comprehend. It was so subtle, so tangential. "It's almost as if nothing is happening at all," he said.

"Maybe that's it," said Ewan. "And *this* is all some kind of mass delusion."

"A delusion so convincing that it fills the churches, and the B&Bs in Bonnybridge, and the morgue slabs with the ones who can't cope with it?" Shell replied quietly.

"Isn't that one definition of a religion?" someone else said. Colin couldn't see who. "Just what we need on this planet is a new religion." Two or three people laughed darkly.

"Religions usually require a measure of blind faith," Dave mused. "This is different. People are reacting to personal experiences here. Private raptures."

"Well, not me," said Ewan. "I've not seen a thing. And neither has my family, or to my knowledge anyone I know."

"Same here," said Dave, and a number of others chorused their agreement. Shell and Deepak looked into their drinks and said nothing. There was a dangerous moment then, that Colin saw with uncomfortable clarity. During that moment any one of them could have pursued the experiences of the group's tacit dissenters, but that would have turned the theoretical into the practical, and, in doing so, crowbarred open the carefully maintained consensus normality that persisted around the table. No-one did. The moment passed and the talk reverted to teasing Ewan about his choices of entertainment.

Shortly after, Paddy touched Colin's arm and asked to go home. He handed her the keys, not wishing to leave this island of camaraderie just yet. In the event, the talkers strove to keep going a little longer but the spirit of the gathering had been undermined, and people started to drift off into the night. Besides, he found himself worrying about Paddy.

When he got home he went straight to the bathroom. By the flaccid way she lay in the cooling water, only her nostrils and mouth breaking the surface, he thought that she had drowned. The way her hair floated like weed. The way her white skin, apart from the dark blot of the tattoo, goose-fleshed. The way her eyes stared, oblivious. Only the rapid puffs of breath steaming the air told him she was alive. That, and the mottled rashes chasing each other across her skin like the shadows of clouds. At first he hoped this effect was a trick of the water and light, but saw that it was too regular. The shifting shapes began at her sternum, and radiated outwards across her breasts and belly, sweeping down her arms and legs to her extremities, and then smoothly back again to the centre. Her face was a confusion of overlapping flushes. Colin burned with questions about this illness – it couldn't be anything else – but he could not talk to her like this.

*

Twenty minutes later Paddy came into the back room where he was leafing through some binders of old work. The blue towelling robe she wore was damp at the collar.

"Can I shoot you?" he asked. "Please."

She was crying, but nodded. "Over here?"

"Yes, the chair's good." He handed her the binder to look at while he set up his gear. "You've changed," he said, noticing that she had slipped a contact sheet out of its plastic pocket.

"I look so young in these," Paddy said with a small laugh. "Look at my hair. And all that make up. What was I like?"

"You were beautiful," Colin said, tightening the locks on his tripod. "But that's not what I'm talking about. You're like a completely different person to the Paddy that – " He hadn't meant to bring it up, but she already knew what was coming. "That left," he finished.

"Well, that's how it happens," he heard her say, as he reached behind the reflectors to flick the lights on. There was a defensive edge to her voice. "Sometimes people appear unrecognisable after a relationship has ended. Like you never knew the real person all that time, or they shed the personality you knew like an unwanted skin." She sounded like she meant it. If it hadn't been for her illness he might even have been convinced.

"That's not what I'm talking about either," he said, sighting through the viewfinder. "It's more subtle than that." He hadn't intended for her to take the robe off, but now it lay on the floor beside the chair he knew that he needed her to be as open to him as possible. The indirect lighting made the sheen on her skin luminescent. The tattoo glistened as if freshly inked. He focussed tight on the tattoo, squeezed off a shot. Tracked up the s-curve of her hip and waist to the well of her navel, took a second.

Paddy sighed. "You always did pay too much attention to the details," she said.

"What do you mean?" A curve of breast obscured by an arm. The hairs at the crook of the elbow sleek with moisture.

"Nothing," she said. "It's just you. The way you look at the world, noticing the tiny things, but never quite aware of the whole picture."

Was that how he came across? Myopic and obsessed with minutiae? He didn't think that was true, it was just that he knew the world at large would roll on whether he noticed it or not – so why bother? But this was straying from the point. This wasn't about him.

"I want to know what it's like," he said. The corner of her mouth twitched with conflicting emotions. He photographed that too.

"I can't tell you," she said. "You wouldn't – "

"I wouldn't understand?" he interrupted.

"I can't explain it. It's like a new kind of weather, or a new note squeezed into the scale, or like a colour no-one's ever seen before. How can you explain something like that?" A bright eye, hazel iris on pure white. Pupil wide and depthless. If he could focus tight enough, Colin thought he might be able to see *it* inside her, looking out. Whatever this thing was that caused her illness.

"Please try," he said. "What do they look like?"

"I don't know," she said. "I never saw anything. One minute I was talking on the phone to my mum, and then – "

"I need to know," he persisted.

"Col," she said. "It's no use. I think it's different for everybody. Maybe some people *do* see little green men, and maybe some see God, and some Yogi-fucking-Bear. But not me. I think whatever it is – whatever *they* are – looks into people and finds something that no-one else has, perhaps the single element that makes them an individual, and then they tweak it to see what happens." There was a weariness in her voice now. He wondered if this illness was killing her.

"I don't know if they are aliens or not," she said, "but I do know they weren't here a month ago – none of this weird shit was happening a month ago – so it's likely isn't it? Whoever they are, I think they are simply curious about humans. They're just giving us a prod and a poke."

He put the camera down. "I envy you," he said.

"Do you? I'm scared. I don't think I'm even human any more."

In the night, when they held each other, the warmth of skin, the strength of muscle and bone, the vitality of two pulses, Colin thought he was convinced that Paddy was still human. What else could she be?

Later when she slept he got out of bed and took a long bath. Eventually the water cooled and his skin wrinkled. When he started to shiver he climbed out, dried off and returned to bed.

*

In the morning Paddy was gone. Really gone this time. He knew it from the moment he woke in an empty bed, but he checked the back room, the living room, the kitchen. In the bathroom the towels were lying in the bath where he had left them the previous night.

Neil Williamson

Even knowing she was gone he went out to look. His street deserted, he instinctively headed towards Great Western Road, despite the fact that at rush hour on a Thursday morning it would be so busy that anyone could vanish instantly amid the traffic and crowd. Except it too was deserted. No cars in motion, no trucks rumbling, no people bustling, shouting, chatting. It was as if the world had been emptied in the night, save for himself. This was what an alien invasion was supposed to be like. Of course, it was just an impression caused by arriving at exactly the wrong moment, and it only lasted an instant or two. Then, as if a hidden switch were thrown, or all the world's traffic lights turned green, a butcher's shop door opened and a young mother emerged with a push chair, quickly followed by others from other shops, doorways and side streets, and two surges of traffic filled the empty road. In seconds the moment had passed, and the world, as far as Colin could tell, was as it always had been.

There was no doubt now that Paddy was gone.

When the first drops of rain arced out of the sky, Colin leaned against the frontage of the newsagent and watched. There was something odd. He looked more closely. These drops, disobeying the usual dynamics of falling liquids, were perfect spheres. In fact they reminded him of nothing less than miniature versions of the glass marbles he had owned as a kid.

He held out a palm. The globes of rain landed in his hand, intact for an instant before bursting and seeping away. Cementing the likeness to marbles in his mind, was the writhing twist of life colouring the centre of each.

Colin wondered if anyone else in the world had noticed that the rain was amber, or if he were the only one touched by the invisible aliens to be allowed to see them.

92

Postcards

In this city the sun draws the palette. Here the buildings, tall smears of sienna and ochre and cream press close around you; the air and the water are depthless, still as anticipation; the people are loud sparks of life, gold and bronze and passionate olive green, living embers of the sun that burn throughout the night. The main streets are rivers of bright noise; shining shop fronts ensnaring tourists herded along their lengths by brash scooter cowboys.

But underneath this reflective skin, a darker, mysterious heart. The real city, hidden piazzas and colonnaded courtyards, half in angled shade, where passage of time fades with the sounds of the mainstream.

I can understand why Rose loved this place so much. I can understand the happiness in her face and in her voice, and in the postcards she sent me with her letters. But I am not at all sure I understand my own reasons for coming here.

*

This was her room. Room 232, Albergo Rapallo. I pause outside for uncertain seconds before sliding the key easily into the lock and letting the door swing open. I enter slowly, not breathing, as if expecting to detect some remnant of her presence. But no, the room is clean and still, permeated with a staleness that comes with disuse.

It is exactly as I expected (*remembered*), maybe a little smaller; video always has a tendency to make things seem larger. It is all here. The single bed, narrow, white sheets stretched tight; basic wooden furniture dark against the faded floral walls; a single mirror filmed with dust catches the late evening light from the window opposite. A door to one side leads to a tiny bathroom, predictably white.

I close the shutters and pull the viewer out of its case, sliding the first disc out of its box (a date, *11/6*, in Rose's scrawl across the label) and into the viewer. I hold it up to my eyes and proceed to relive my first impressions of this city.

The scene is this same room, a different time of day, two months ago. The shutters are open wide and the room seems a whole lot brighter. The camera pans slowly, a little jerkily, around in a circle from the window; taking in the bed (holding her as yet unpacked suitcases), the bathroom, the door, the mirror and finally the window again which it approaches to obtain a view of the empty side street below. The soundtrack consists of distant street noises overlaid by Rose's breathing until she remembers to speak.

Well, here I am. I just got in twenty minutes ago. This is my room. It ain't much, but as it's going to be my home for the next three months I guess I'd better get used to it. At least it's within walking distance of the Galleria. Good job I asked for a room with a view, Huh?

The camera draws back into the room, the picture blurring for a second as the autofocus adjusts to the difference in light levels. One more sweep around the room finishes up straight on the mirror so that she is focusing on her own image. Keeping the camera still, she moves to one side so that I can see her whole face. Given a grainy quality by the dust on the mirror it is pale and drawn from the flight and the hassle of the Italian traffic between the airport and the hotel. Her pallor only serves to underline the darkness of her eyes and of the dense spill of tight curls that frames her face. A half embarrassed smile curls her lip as she seems to be searching for something to say.

Guess that's about all for now. I'd better tell you again how much I'll miss you just to set your mind at,...

A knock at the door draws her gaze for a second. When she returns her attention to the mirror her brow is knitted in puzzlement. Arching her eyebrows, a facial shrug, and smiling wryly, she finishes off.

I'll bet that's room service wanting to know where I want the jacuzzi put in. Better love you and leave you, eh? Take care Mickey. Ciao bambino.

She blows a kiss, affecting a caricature Latin pout and takes her finger from the trigger of the camera. The viewer fills with static.

Of the disks she sent me from this city, this is the one to which I return most often, pausing and slow searching her dust filmed image countless times. For what? I don't know. Perhaps it is because this is the only one of the disks in which Rose is actually seen, and so these pictures are the very last I have of her. Perhaps it is because this was the last time I could be sure of her sincerity when she said she loved me. Perhaps it is because, for both of these reasons, this is the one of her postcards that hurts me most to experience again and again. Replacing the viewer in its case, I go to bed. When sleep comes I dream in freeze frame.

*

I take the viewer out with me early before it gets too warm for tramping around the streets. The second disk is a haphazard tourist's guide to the city. It comprises little more than a series of location shots of landmarks. For want of a better guide, I am content to follow in Rose's footsteps.

I spend the morning treading the same vias, taking in the views from the same pontes, sweating for a Perrier and succumbing at the same corner cafe-bars. Rose's dialogue tends to centre on how much she is looking forward to working at the Galleria. They had given her a couple of days to settle in before she was expected to actually turn up for work. Her boss was to be some Dutchman named van Bosen but she hadn't met him yet.

From the top of one of the taller square towers off Via Ghibellina which offers 'an unparalleled vista' across the city (for only 4000 lira), the camera zooms in on a somewhat convoluted arrangement of red rooftops away from the main streets, quite far in the distance. *Look at that. It's so unusual. Must be some kind of church, I think.* I have never been able to discern the object of her amazement from the pictures but actually standing here, I think I can just perceive a spire in that area. It is hard to make out due to a localised shimmering effect which I can only attribute to a trick of the heat and the distance. I had assumed that Rose never found it because it did not appear in any of the other postcards; or at least if she did, she did not have her camera with her. This disk ends with the view of the river from the middle of the elaborate Ponte Alle Grazia. Something about the steady, unrelenting flow of the waters unsettles me. It carries a disturbing inevitability.

*

By two the sun is high and has bludgeoned many of the tourists into following the citizens indoors. Unusually I find myself unaffected by the thick heat, in fact I am enjoying the sudden quiet of the streets. However, despite my sunglasses, I can feel a headache building from the brightness of the sunlight which has taken on a quality of diamantine hardness as the day has

96

progressed. I stop at a cafe and order a coffee, sitting well back in the shade of the faded canopy. There are only one or two other customers but still my order seems to be taking an age to arrive. I use the time to swap the disk in the viewer for the third one in the sequence and begin watching it.

This one is taken over dinner following Rose's first day at work at the Galleria. It is a noisy affair and in it, her voice a little slurred, she introduces me to her new colleagues, a confusing jumble of names and faces, all laughing. A scene sparking with bonhomie, and although I cannot see Rose, I can easily pick out her laugh, hear how much she is sharing in the enjoyment of the evening. I remember when I first received this disk I felt a small amount of jealousy on seeing that she could be enjoying herself so much with these strangers. Without me. How long had it been since she laughed like that in my company? At the time I dismissed the feeling but on each viewing since I have felt that hollow pit in my stomach more and more acutely.

This is Gianfranco. This is Roberto, he's in antiquities. This is Cecilia and Iria; and here's my boss, Tomas van Bosen.

I don't acknowledge the waiter when my coffee finally arrives; my attention is fixed on the viewer. I sip slowly as I become engrossed again in this, my favourite game: trawling each visage, wondering if this is the one or that is the one and not knowing for sure that it has happened at all. All I have is a feeling born of too many late-night phone calls to her hotel that went unanswered, of some subtle change in her demeanour when we did talk – not in the things she said so much as in the things she did not. She stayed in that hotel for no longer than six weeks, and neither they nor the Galleria are able (or willing) to tell me where she moved to.

I strain to hear the soundtrack, trying to analyze the babel of conversation that perhaps I might pick up some spoken clue that I have missed each time before. It is impossible, though. Intelligible phrases bob to the surface of the conversation only rarely and since the language is mostly

Italian, the integral translator of the viewer is reduced to making guesses at context.

One of the men, Gianfranco, suddenly reaches down to the floor and saying, '*Hey, Salvatore,*' lifts a small spindly dog up onto his lap. The camera focuses on its pointed face, all blunted yellow teeth and stringy hair. It is obviously old. Its eyes closed to slits, weeping at the corners; its nose dry and scabbed; its tongue a dripping slab of pink-grey flesh lolling out of the left side of its mouth. Gianfranco starts feeding it scraps from his plate which it sniffs at suspiciously and swallows feebly.

In the background two children run in, at first unseen by the camera but clearly heard, *Salvatore, Salvatore!* The general chatter subsides into a smattering of patronising comments and chuckles of the kind generally reserved for children. They approach the table, coming into view, a perfectly matched pair of sisters aged, I would guess, about nine and six. Straight dark hair, big chocolate eyes, smooth round faces set in identically serious expressions. Dresses of thin green cotton hang loosely from their shoulders. The elder walks up to Gianfranco's chair and thrusts out her palms accusingly at him. His expression seems to be confused between amusement and consternation, as he places the dog in her arms. She clutches the animal to her body and then turns her face to the camera. Her gaze is directed straight into the lens and is sullen and petulant, and irrationally or not I cannot help but feel it as threatening, carrying a degree of malevolence. Quietly but clearly I hear Rose's voice, apologetic, *Oh, I'm sorry.* The disk ends.

I dig out some coins to pay for the coffee and splash them into the saucer provided. The waiter comes as I stand up to go and lifting the saucer, stares at the pattern of currency like a haruspex. I wonder what omens he sees there. He scoops the coins fluidly into his pouch, bestowing on me a look which I cannot decipher but which feels most like sympathy, before retreating inside. I follow the assured path of the river back to my hotel.

*

I spend the rest of the day back in that room shuttered tight against the hard light, thinking about Rose and the fourth disk until evening. This one is a mystery, a confused montage of disconnected shots that make no sense. There is no label and no commentary as such, and there was no usual letter with it when it arrived, which was about a week after I last heard from her. Nothing to confirm that she sent it at all in fact. Nevertheless I know it was from her. I have only once viewed it all the way through.

A change of light. The noise of conversation drifting up from the street below and then passing by. It is enough to break my lethargy, forcing me to replay the final disk.

*

It is dark, quiet. I can hear echoes of footsteps as if in a tunnel. The view emerges into a wide courtyard, lit only intermittently by the stars in the heavily clouded sky above. A hulking building dominates the courtyard but it cannot be made out in detail. I can hear the crunch of gravel beneath feet. There is movement in the shadows ahead and the view approaches the building.

A wall of tiles. Smooth and shiny, the designs on them are hard to make out at first, but a break in the clouds shows them to be bright and colourful although crudely rendered; and it seems, all different. A voice, low and indistinct causes the view to turn sharply and look along the wall. A figure in shadow beckons and the words *Come, come. This way*, can be heard clearly spoken in English but thick with accent. Somewhere, a dog begins to bark.

An arched doorway, plain and unembossed. A large wooden door which in this light has a greenish tint and a sheen

99

Neil Williamson

of slickness, stands ajar. A hand reaches forward and pushes it
open. The view enters slowly. Darkness. Somewhere behind
something is said of which the only word which can be heard is
Pazzi. The translator provides an interpretation: pazzi = mad,
insane (m/f. pl.)

The interior is almost entirely dark. The floor is flagstoned
but that is all that can be seen. There is a very dim light which
has no apparent point of origin. The view appears to be moving
in a straight line but there is no indication of passage of time
other than the movement over the cracks in the stone floor.
There is no sound whatsoever. Eventually, a dark and heavy
curtain. Pause. It is drawn quickly aside.

Flash. After straining to make out detail in the previous
darkness, the sudden brightness makes me blink painfully. It
lasts only an instant and my eyes have difficulty adjusting to
the picture again. At first it seems that the scene is the same, but
as my eyes begin to make out the details once more I realise we
are now in a darkened room. Two figures lie in a bed, one is
asleep. His companion lies still watching him, her cheeks
glistening. This scene is only on the screen for a few seconds and
I am unable to recognise them.

Flash. Walking up an aisle between the seats on an
aeroplane. The plane is large and half of the seats are empty.
The view moves up the aisle looking at the backs of the
passengers' heads, alternating smoothly from side to side as
if looking for someone in particular. There. Eight or nine rows
ahead, on the left by the window. The top of a woman's head,
curls of dark hair, staring out of the window which is streaked
with rain. As the view approaches, the head starts to turn.

Flash. A piece of dusty, rubble-strewn waste ground. The
view starts close up on a stringy piece of rotting meat lying
on the ground and then draws out. Two skinny dogs, horribly
thin, approach from different directions and sniff around the
piece of carcass, pawing it and eying each other with suspicion.
Suddenly they erupt into a fit of snarling and fighting, dragging

100

the meat around, pulling it to bits.

Flash. A deeply shadowed tropical forest glade, an explosion of green. As the view moves through it, branches, lianas and broad leaves are pushed out of the way. The view tilts upwards into the high canopy of the trees and only feet away on a broad branch is a bird to which I cannot put a name, but is of such exquisite beauty that it makes me gasp. Its long elegant feathers, all colours, trail from the branch and the glorious comb on its head shimmers and waves as it cocks its head inquisitively in my direction. Without warning as if in reaction to some noise, it is gone in a rainbow cloud of feathers, leaving only the gently waving branch.

Flash. A fountain in a meticulously tended garden. The centrepiece of the fountain is vague but appears to be serpentine in form. A fine mist hangs in the air. The view turns away from the fountain and approaches an arbour. Trees and trailing plants grow thickly providing almost complete shade although a few stray beams of sunlight do manage to get through to illuminate a life sized statue of a boy. Getting closer it turns out to be beautifully rendered in white marble, its head to one side, arms outstretched in a gesture that conveys both release and welcoming in equal parts. The gently curved face emphasises this with an expression which could be profound sadness or sublime happiness. The eyes cry hard mossy tears.

Flash. Grey gravel at the base of the tiled wall, a different section of the exterior. The view focuses on one tile in particular. It looks like a bird. The soundtrack has suddenly returned. I can hear a bell tolling loudly and continuously nearby, and beneath it the sound of a woman sobbing.

Static.

*

Sunset is a transition of hot fluidity bathing the city in a slow wave of deepening light; a laval wash changing the cadence of life. I stand on the Ponte Santa Trinita feeling as much as watching the flow of the carmine tinted waters beneath my feet, as relentless and single-purposed as blood. Carrying over the water, sounds of conversation, laughter, music weave through the still warm air, heralding the awakening of the city's nightlife. Street lights are flickering on as a group approach the bridge from the shadowed streets to my left. There are six or seven of them, loud and garrulous. The city is a bright theatre for those who know how to use it but I can only stand in the shadows and observe. Soon others pass me in small groups, twos and threes, becoming a flow, a river, kinetic and purposeful. I am caught between these two streams, the calm at the centre of the turbulence. Between the inevitable progress of the waters and the life-force of the people of the city, I am becalmed. I cannot remember my purpose.

I came here charged with determination following Rose's last letter, the one in which she drew a red line under our stuttering relationship. My imagination dwelled on moments, words, expressions, inflamed them with suspicion. I arrived here, when it was too late, *knowing* that she would change her mind when she saw me face to face. I have become a master of the art of self-delusion.

Bestilled here I see some of the truth reflected around me in the faces and the wetly lapping waves, but still I continue to hope. Since my arrival I have been putting off the inevitable, going to the Galleria, torn between the need to see her and the dread of seeing her with someone else. Still unresolved, I let the flow of life sweep me into the lights of the city.

I approach the large doors of the Galleria with a half-felt relief that it has closed to the public for the evening. I should have realised it would be. There are one or two lighted windows, however, high in the marbled facade. Perhaps people working late. Maybe one of them is Rose. I force myself up the steps and find the heavy doors unlocked. Inside, a mosaic floor leads away down an echoing hallway, plaster walls studded with dark wooden doors. At the end a staircase rises into shadow.

To my left a neat little man regards me from behind a desk.

"Hello." His accent is soupy but his intonation is clear. It is not a question, not 'Can I help you?' or 'What are you doing here?', just a casual greeting. He peers at me with needle-sharp eyes, light from his desk lamp glinting off the half lenses of his steel-rimmed glasses and the silver buttons of his precise grey uniform. His expression is inscrutable amid the leathery mapwork of his face.

"I am looking for Rose Christie," I begin, a little unsettled. "She works here." He continues to look at me, not speaking, so that I begin to wonder whether he has understood despite his initial greeting. As I open my mouth to repeat myself, he finally speaks.

"Si, Rosa." His voice has a swimming, hypnotic effect so that I have to concentrate hard on what he is saying to make the words register in my mind. "Not here. What you seek, not here. La Cappella dei Pazzi." He gets up out of his seat and leads the way towards the exit, "Come. With me, come." I am transfixed with astonishment both at his reaction to my request and at his use of the word 'pazzi' in connection with Rose. At the doors he turns. His face shows a measure of concern.

"Come, now. Please." Entranced, I follow him out into the street. At first I have to run to catch up with him, as he bustles quickly around a corner. I am still amazed at him. Is he going to take me to Rose rather than give directions to a foreigner with no knowledge of the labyrinthine innards of the city? Struggling to keep up with him I try to find out more but his only reply is to urge me ever onwards. We scuttle along streets and narrow alleys which suddenly open out into broad piazzas, up and down short winding flights of steps. As we penetrate deeper into the heart of the city, the sounds of living are pushed into the background until we are left with only the clacking of our own feet on the stony ground.

Turning sharply to the left we enter an arched tunnel mouth, almost completely dark, and I can barely make out the grey figure of the porter ahead of me. We pass through in what seems like minutes, but as we emerge into the gravelled courtyard beyond I am amazed to see that though we had entered the tunnel maybe an hour after sunset, the sun is already high in the sky causing the tiles on the walls of the church building directly ahead to shimmer like molten glass. La Cappella dei Pazzi.

At the porter's beckoning I approach. Up close the tiles are dazzling, beautiful and garish; simplistic, each conveying its own definitive message; and in concert an overall feeling of vital translucency. Looking at individual designs I can see dogs, cats, buildings, stick men, women and children, families, houses, crosses, stars, flowers and trees, the moon in a hundred phases, the sun also, eclipses and novae. The colours are bold and primary. The variations are limitless and the tiles cover the entire exterior of the chapel, even the roof and spire. There are no windows. Reaching out my hand I find that the tiles are warm to the touch.

"Micheli. Hurry, please." The porter is beckoning again, this time towards the doorway of the chapel. The plain arch frames a wooden door, shiny with green paint, which stands ajar. He motions for me to enter. "Now you will see." As I penetrate the cool dark and the door swings behind me I wonder: Micheli? How did he know my name?

*

The flagstones stretch out in front of me, flat and hard beneath my feet. The temperature is much lower than outside and I fail to suppress a shiver as I walk forward. There is no sound, neither of my breathing nor of my footfalls, as I progress down what I assume to be an aisle although I cannot see anything to the sides. I continue walking, one foot after the other and time passes.

Eventually the curtain I have been expecting comes into view and I stop before it. It is of a thick velvety material the colour of old wine. I grasp the edge, feeling the ancient cloth luxuriant in my fingers, and pull it aside.

Flash. A wide lawn stretches in front of a large house, paving winds from the door of the house down past a stately pond. The lawn is surrounded by beautiful borders of carefully nurtured bedding plants and shrubs, a number of small fruit trees provide shade. A man comes out of the house and surveys the scene, happy, obviously pleased with his garden. As he walks down the path everything behind him withers and decays, weeds run rampant over the lawn, the fruit falls rotten to the ground before the trees themselves crack and topple. The man walks on oblivious. The weeds have choked the lawn completely and large patches of brown earth appear, the pond grows still and stagnates, a miasmal scum spreading over the surface. Only when the man reaches the end of the path does he turn.

Flash. A coal fire blazes in a grate. An old ornate fireplace surrounds it, the mantel littered with ornaments and objects: a glass carriage clock, a set of tiny nested Russian dolls, a pile of bills and a brass letter opener, a crystal vase holding a few ageing daffodils, and a scattered pile of Polaroid photographs. In each of the shots a man is positioned as if with another person who has vanished from the frame. As if in slow motion the pictures topple from the mantel and float onto the fire. They buckle and blister before being consumed.

Flash. A brass birdcage on a high stand, covered by a torn cloth, thin with age. A group of men stand beneath it craning their necks to see inside. Through the rents in the cloth tantalising glimpses are had of bright plumage, and a crested silhouette is discernable. A breath of wind tugs the cloth away to reveal the exotic bird which I recognise from Rose's fourth disk. The cage door is opened and the bird flies gracefully out of the window.

Flash. There is a flat rock at the place where two wide rivers meet and then diverge again. One of the rivers is slow but forceful, its waters dark and calming. The other is a bright torrent, teeming with fish, dragonflies swooping gracefully through clouds of

Neil Williamson

midges. Birds wade in its less turbulent shallows amid a swathe
of reeds and river flowers. An otter drags itself onto the flat rock.
It has been swimming for a while along the edge of the slow river
and it is weary. It must decide whether to brave the tiring, busy
waters to its left or to return to the calm and gentle repose of the
river to the right. Understanding, I will its choice, and it dives
under, flicking its tail as it goes. A few drops of sparkling liquid
hang like crystals in the air.

Flash. Lying on the ground I can feel gravel pressing into
my face. I raise my head slowly to face the wall of tiles. The glare
hurts my eyes until I get used to it and here I see them. Two tiles.
One depicts an exquisite bird in flight. The other, a stylised otter,
a smudge of brown with black dots for eyes, swimming in a
scintillating azure stream.

*

Madness can be a small thing, a cobweb veil obscuring what we
know to be right. In the Cappella dei Pazzi we were allowed for a
time to lift the veil. To see clearly. When Rose moved here I
cursed the distance, but the distance was there long before she
set foot on Italian soil. I remain a master of the art of self-
delusion but at least, deep down, I know I am doing it.

106

Softly Under Glass

The Grace-girl's portfolio lay open on the table between their espresso cups.

"So am I right or am I right?" Maria was saying. Hugo wasn't sure. Personally he found the images rather bleak and disturbing, although he could not say why since they were somewhat indistinct in this reduced format. He realised that he could not even tell what medium had been used to create them.

"I don't know, Maria." He flicked through the folio. "I'd have to see the originals under decent light. How were these done? Some kind of photo-montage? Or is it a computer thing." The way he sneered this made obvious his views of the role of electronic media in the world of art.

"None of the above," said Maria. "Or maybe all of the above. I don't know. The artist is vague about her techniques. She *says* they are paintings but I've seen the originals and I'll be damned if I can see any brush strokes." She sipped her coffee and watched for his reaction. Hugo turned the pages again, pretending to consider. He didn't like these pictures; they were odd, they made him feel uncomfortable. All the same, personal tastes notwithstanding, he was in the business of giving the public what they wanted; or more exactly, what people like Maria and himself persuaded them that they wanted. Maria had a good sense of the mood of the art world and a knack of discovering just the right person for the times. As an agent she was prolific, and as a barometer she was rarely wrong. Maybe this girl's work did have that shock/sadness quality that was currently in vogue. Hugo knew that if he passed up this offer, someone else would be given the option.

"You'd better arrange a meeting then," he said as casually as he could manage.

"Fine. Friday at eleven." Maria's smile was enigmatic. It smacked of manipulation.

*

Alison Grace was by no means the embodiment of her name. She shuffled into the gallery like so much grey flotsam dragged along in Maria's purposeful wake. Her clothes were smart, but muted in colour, and hung on her tiny bony frame as if it consisted entirely of wire hangers. Her hair, clean and perfunctorily cut, framed a pale angular face in which the heavily lidded eyes were cast at the floor. Hugo rose to meet the women, smiling. He felt that measure of superiority, familiar to him when meeting artists, as he straightened the cuffs of his mauve suit, which he wore today over a commanding green roll-neck. Maria made introductions and he extended his hand exposing a glint of Rolex gold. The artist's hand was warm and dry, and gripped more firmly than he expected. Those heavy lids fluttered up to reveal intense green eyes which immediately captured his own gaze and held it. Her voice was a soft sound punctuated by *tuts* and *clicks*, and it put Hugo in mind of feathers and brittle bones.

"Glad to meet you Mister de Villiers." She said it with an upward inflection, like a question. "I'm honoured that you have taken an interest in my work." The woman's unsettling presence, belied by her appearance, caused the glaze of Hugo's composure to crack just a fraction. He looked to Maria for help, but was met only by an amused half-smile. He forced his attention back to the artist. *Ridiculous*. Why should he feel threatened by *this*? Almost immediately he felt his accustomed feeling of superiority return. He smiled his standard radiant smile.

"Gallerie de Villiers is always eager to promote original works." He waved his arm in an expansive arc. The woman's face remained impassive, showing no sign of being impressed.

"Sarah." Hugo, a little annoyed, looked over to his assistant. "Miss Grace's pieces arrived this morning, yes?"

"Yes, Mister de Villiers. They've been unpacked and are waiting in the rear office."

"Fine." He took the artist lightly by the arm. "Come, let us discuss how best to display your work." The pair followed closely by Maria headed towards the back of the building. Over his shoulder he said, "Oh, and Sarah? Coffee."

*

By mid-afternoon the gallery was closed. The walls of the prime exhibition area had been cleared and were now home to the twelve pictures. The discussions over the mounting sequence between Hugo, Alison and Maria were earnest, bordering on argument, and were joined in equal voice by Sarah and even the receptionist, Eloise.

Hugo paced back and forth, becoming irascible as his authoritatively voiced contributions were heeded less and less. Alison Grace stood back quietly in contemplation as Maria, Sarah and Eloise raised their voices to stress their own versions of the right, the *only*, way to display this collection.

These pictures certainly engendered opinion. Hugo had to

109

Neil Williamson

admit that they had power. Only a fraction of it had come over in the photographs Maria had showed him, but standing here he could not deny that there was some poignancy of subject and composition, some subtlety of technique in each that was at once enthralling and beautiful and disturbing, such that in a few cases he could not look at them for more than a few seconds. And even now looking at the entire collection he could not see how these pictures were created, although certainly they were all products of the same method. Each, simply framed and bordered in white, had the textural appearance of parchment with the clarity of a photographic image. The central images appeared in each case to have been arranged in front of a video picture. This backing image was distorted in some way so that the original subject all but lost its identity: either by enlargement so that only a small segment was visible, or by blurring due to motion, or in some cases by overlaying different aspects of the same image on each other. The backgrounds were tantalisingly incomplete and carried an implicit link to the central images, a hint at meaning. But these central images themselves were even more enigmatic. They were photographic in quality but of impossible constructions. No, they were not photographs, not even of sculptures; and neither were they photo-montages or computer composites. The artist denied using any of these techniques although she did admit to the use of video to provide the backgrounds.

Each picture, although uniform in style, evoked a unique emotional response in Hugo; and an entirely different set of responses, it seemed, in the others. *This one*: an alabaster hand cups a pile of coins. Some glitter brightly, gold and silver; others dulled, tarnished and chipped; still others in rusting pieces, turning to a fine metallic powder which slips through the clutching fingers and cascades onto a polished silver tray beneath. The tray reflects the images of a group of people but the growing pile of powder is quickly covering them over. The background is black and white, apparently in the process

110

of losing definition. A large pyramid shape is dissolving into monochrome static. In its centre the form of a stylised ellipse can just be made out holding a vertically off-centre circle within it. Lines or rays appear to be radiating from the shape.

Hugo found that he had a certain fascination with this picture although at the same time he found it ultimately frustrating. Maria and Eloise seemed to feel the same way about it although Sarah spent only a few moments at it before moving on.

This one: A sylph-like female figure kneels on an old mattress, naked, her skin has a pearly sheen. Her head is raised and turned in order to look behind her in the direction of the background which is a wall of human flesh, a composite image of all manner of sexual configurations in which the defining edges are smeared, joining to form a single heaving body. She has beautiful wings of silver feathers but they are tarnishing and falling away. One hand is handcuffed to the mattress; beside the other is a silver key. She could free herself but she is rapt in the images behind her.

Maria was very taken with this piece, and to a lesser extent, so was Eloise. Hugo hated this picture, and said as much, but found excuses to return to it. In truth he could not deny that it was beautiful, capturing a note of transcendent eroticism which was hypnotic.

This one: A man sits in a room, a book is open on his lap. He is cowering in the chair, apparently screaming. The reason for this appears to be the eyes. Staring, unblinking eyes watch the man from all around the room. From the walls, from the swirls in the pattern on the Persian rug on the floor, from the end of the door knob, from the centre of each bloom in a vase of daisies, from each numeral on the mantle clock, from the studs in the arms of his leather wingback chair, from the open pages of the discarded book in his lap, and outstretched before him in horror, from the palms and fingertips of his own hands. The blurred, sepia-toned image behind this depicts what could be a figure running, a dark arc where its head would be, as if looking round frantically.

For some reason this one unsettled Hugo most, striking a chord of familiarity deep within him, the others seemed only marginally affected by it.

Hugo asked Alison about the motivation that led her to create these, and she told him that they were portraits, after a fashion. She would not elaborate further.

The arguments went on. Eventually it became clear that they were not going to arrive at any decision. Maria sighed with exasperation,

"There is no balance here. We need a central piece around which to base the exhibition, but none of us seem to be able to choose the same one."

Hugo started to say that this was what he had been saying all along, when Alison spoke. "Then I shall have to start work on a new piece."

Hugo made to protest that the gallery could not be held indefinitely, but she cut him short. "I will have it here by Monday morning." She turned to Sarah, "Will you arrange a cab for me." Sarah made the call and then escorted the lady to the door. When the girl returned she was clutching a piece of paper bearing the artist's address.

"She wants me to sit for the picture," she said.

*

The artist delivered the picture as promised. Sarah helped her bring it in and unwrapped it herself with eager hands before carrying it over and placing it against the wall. Stepping back to view it properly she shared a thrilled look with Alison Grace. The others stood rapt, silent for long moments. The picture was truly striking.

Foreground was a woman, tall and naked standing ankle deep in a pool of water. Her arms extended vertically above her head entwining round each other, fingers splayed, stretching into slender branches, dividing and spreading to form a leafy canopy which hung down to the water level. The trailing ends of the branches floated on the surface of the pool. The canopy was not so dense as to completely obscure the woman, rather the branches cast alluring patterns of light and shade on her limbs and torso; only her face was completely masked. Nestling within the leaves were heavy fruit, apparently ruddy with ripeness. Under closer inspection though their skins were seen to be transparent, each enclosing a huddled embryo in a clear, viscous fluid. The video background was a grainy picture of a human zygote in an advanced stage of division.

Sarah hugged herself. "I never knew," she said quietly. Her face was aglow with wonder and when she exchanged another thrilled glance with the artist her eyes were bright, brimming with secrets.

Hugo was almost overwhelmed by the strength of the picture. It was bold and to the point; despite its graceful beauty, it shone with an almost palpable quality of life and well-being. He was the first to break the awed silence.

"Yes. Oh, yes," he whispered. "This is the one."

Amongst the others, Sarah's picture was a natural focus, and the sequence of the rest seemed to resolve itself naturally.

*

That night, Hugo dreamt. As the dream began he recognised it as a recurring one, but as always he could not remember how it ended.

In his dream he was standing before an enormous mirror. He stood for a long time admiring himself. His clothes, his hair, his face: everything looked good. There was no mistaking him; he was a figure of distinction.

Then his face began to melt away.

*

Neil Williamson

Three flights up. In this heat. Hugo paused to wipe the film of sweat from his face and neck with a paisley patterned handkerchief, damp from frequent use, and then resumed his upward labour in the direction of the girl's studio. He paused again outside her door, long enough to smooth his slightly ruffled appearance before ringing the bell.

The exhibition had fared better than Hugo could ever have expected. Word of mouth had spread quickly leading to daily attendances which bordered on the amazing. Five weeks later and the numbers showed no sign of dropping off. Sarah's picture had proved very popular and had sold immediately. Nearly half of the others were spoken for as well. Maria wanted Hugo to extend the exhibition and he was in no position to argue, so they tried to persuade Alison Grace to produce more of her unique art. She had seemed reluctant, protesting that it was difficult to find suitable subjects. After the results of Sarah's sitting they had all offered themselves, but she had turned down Maria and Eloise flat. She had looked long at Hugo however, as if weighing him up, before eventually assenting.

Waiting for the door to be answered, Hugo preened himself. He knew he was looking good, from the careful arrangement of his hair, to the even bronze shade of his skin, to carefully selected couture. He felt a tremor of anticipation. Maria had hardly spoken to him since Alison had chosen him. Eloise vented her own frustration on Sarah, although Sarah was doing a good job of ignoring her.

Hugo was discovering a quiet affection for Sarah since the advent of their association with Alison Grace. She was by far the more capable and conscientious of the two gallery assistants, and had a pleasant demeanour with the clients. He was beginning to find that he enjoyed having her around.

Now that he was aware of what they represented, Hugo privately considered the existing pictures obvious and vulgar, although he had the diplomacy not to say so publicly while the crowds were still queuing outside his door. In the cases of most

114

of the pictures the artist showed herself to be an astute judge of character, and he guessed that she must have picked up on some kind of biological indication of Sarah's pregnancy to create her portrait. Even if Sarah had not been aware herself, Alison Grace was obviously attuned to reading the signs and had successfully conveyed them symbolically on her strange canvas. Again Hugo felt anticipation ripple through him. If an emotional portrait of someone like Sarah could evoke such regard, then what would a likeness of Hugo?

The apartment was not what he had anticipated of Alison Grace. He had been expecting dim rooms crowded with old things, an undisturbed sense of dowdiness and antique clutter. Instead he found the rooms spacious and decorated in an ultra-modern fashion. There was a sparseness which accentuated the expense at which the place had been furnished; each piece of furniture precisely chosen to complement the whole.

Alison Grace ushered him quickly through the apartment to the studio at the back. This too took Hugo by surprise. Rather than an empty bare-boarded attic room bathed in natural light, he discovered that this studio was more akin to a living room. A comfortable looking armchair upholstered in black material sat in the centre of the room, a low-wattage lamp on the floor providing illumination. She motioned for him to sit, which he did. The wall facing the chair was dominated by a large blank television screen. The screen was linked to a digital video camera mounted on a tripod, which Alison was now adjusting. As Hugo twisted round to see what she was doing the low glass table directly in front of the chair appeared on the screen. Beside the camera stood another tripod, this one holding a curious metal frame.

Hugo was becoming nervous. The artist had said nothing since he had arrived. As if sensing this, she looked up from her preparations with a sudden smile which threw him with its warmth.

"Nearly ready," she said, again with an inflection so that he was not sure if she was trying to put him at ease or asking if *he* was ready. The words spoken in her strangely hollow little voice did little to relax him.

She brought over a square bundle wrapped in waxed paper and set it on the table in front of him. Hugo could see that she had donned a pocketed apron and was wearing thin gloves like a surgeon's. She deftly unwrapped the package to reveal what looked like a solid block of green tinted glass. Then she produced a long bladed scalpel from one of the apron's pockets and proceeded to slice the block into three unequal pieces as easily as if it were cheese. She carried the smallest portion, barely a slice, over to the camera where she wrapped it like paper over the lens. The picture on the screen dissolved into a swimming blue static. The second portion, she took to the framework. Here she teased and worked the stuff into a thin sheet which she stretched over the metal like a translucent canvas.

All this she did silently and with the tiniest of motions, which served to increase Hugo's discomfort further. At last, from the floor she picked up two items; a wooden paint brush and a jar of water, and said, "I am ready to begin, Mister de Villiers. If you'd just like to relax and take it in your hands."

Hugo was unsure what she meant. This whole arrangement was so far removed from his expectations that he did not know what to think any more. Alison indicated the remaining block of glass with her brush. Understanding, Hugo reached out and picked it up.

The glass was cool and hard to the touch. It was weighty and the sharp edges cut into his fingers a little until he found a way to hold it comfortably. The artist dipped her brush into the water, flicking off the excess drips on the edge of the jar. Hugo looked up expectantly, his lips forming the words, *What now?*, but Alison cut him off,

"You are a man who likes to surround himself with fine things, Mister de Villiers." Question or statement? Hugo managed to answer, "Yes."

"Fine clothes, fine home, fine car, fine people and of course,

116

the finest art in your gallery." She was staring intently at him now, her brush poised over the transparent sheet. As she continued Hugo noticed that her voice had taken on a thin whispering edge.

"Because only the very finest things can complement your own refined person. Is that not so?"

As he was about to reply, he noticed that the glass in his hands was getting warm, softer, malleable. Before he knew it his hands had sunk into the surface and been enveloped. A sound, 'Ah', came from the artist. He looked back in her direction in alarm. Her eyes were closed and she had begun to paint; clear water in delicate, purposeful strokes on clear canvas.

Hugo tried to pull his hands free but they were held tightly. He stood up trying to shake the glass off but with no success. In fact the glass was flowing quickly up his arms, freezing them, and was beginning to encase his torso and neck.

"It can be really quite pleasant if you relax," said the artist, "but you'll end up hurting yourself if you move around."

He was robbed of that option by the time his hips and then knees were smoothly covered by the liquid glass. As the substance rippled up his face, the wall screen began to flicker and images started to ghost in and out of the static. It was impossible to tell what they were because they were gone and replaced by new ones within seconds. To the side he could see that the sheet Alison was painting on had gained a measure of opacity and was taking on the appearance of parchment with each additional brush stroke.

Then his attention was dragged away and captured by the figure which materialised before him. He recognised it immediately. It was him. An exact replica of himself, dressed exactly the same way and looking into a hand held mirror. It was looking very pleased with itself, beaming his famous smug smile. The reason for this soon became apparent as he became aware of the presence of a crowd of people. From his frozen situation he could not see any of them as they all seemed to be keeping just beyond the limits of his vision, but this simulacrum Hugo was well aware of them, well aware of their attention of which it was obviously the centre. Inside the glass, Hugo could almost hear the whispered comments of admiration and watched as the replica's smile broadened still further. Suddenly the figures came into view and formed a kneeling semicircle around his double. They were elegant people, expensively dressed, an air of importance about them; and their faces were featureless curved silver. His image let the hand holding the mirror hang by his side, choosing to gaze instead into the faces of his admirers and seeing himself from a dozen angles. The video wall held a picture of a vase of cheap plastic flowers reflected as if between two mirrors so that the image multiplied and receded infinitely. A constant flurry of movement in the corner of his vision was the artist painting away feverishly. The sheet was now nearly fully opaque but Hugo could just make out dark outlines through it.

Hugo's eyes widened in their prison as the colour began to fade from the replica, although not from the reflections. It carried on admiring itself even as its beautiful clothes unravelled thread by thread and fell away from its pale body. Hugo, unable to look away, began to mutter to himself that he was imagining this, that it was some sort of hallucination; but something was tugging at his memory, something he recognised. The scene became increasingly familiar as the grey skin began to bubble and melt around the obliviously smiling face. Hugo moaned loudly as he recognised his nightmare. The skin was now flowing like wax, smoothing over the features, falling in heavy droplets onto the floor. The details of the entire head were slowly erased. All that was left was a featureless outline of a man bearing the most superficial of smiles.

As the mirror-faced people turned slowly away, Hugo began to scream, his body shaking violently inside its transparent skin until the glass cracked, frosted and burst away from his body in a crystal shower, lacerating his clothes, leaving traceries of blood on his hands and face. His scream died into heaving sobs as the tableau before him faded quickly and the wall screen image was swamped once more by static.

He cast wildly around the room. He was alone; the artist was gone, her easel empty.

*

The artist passed among her admirers, handing out champagne and receiving complements in exchange. Some of her guests were still seated in front of the viewing window, looking through into the empty studio, apparently in contemplation of the piece, some were reviewing the video footage of the crucial moments, others were standing around engaged in earnest debate. In the course of her journey she overheard comments,

"...this one was much more invigorating, don't you think? The girl last time was far too passive..."

"...I don't agree. I found her acceptance much more satisfying than his denial..."

"...it's the frisson created by the confrontation between the subject and their subconscious that is so exciting..."

Maria approached and took a glass from Alison's tray. She held it aloft and tipped it towards the artist.

"One of your best, I think."

Alison looked abashed. "Well, I don't know. I was quite pleased with the way it turned out."

"Nonsense. It was genius. A very powerful piece." Maria squeezed her protégée's arm lightly in encouragement. "Really."

"He was a good subject. You found him for me."

"Yes I did, didn't I. Poor Hugo. I wonder what he'd say if he knew he was a work of art."

Well Tempered

"January," Rosemary shouted, glancing at the kitchen clock. "I want you sitting at that piano when the instructor arrives."

Of course, the last place she looked was the music room. January was perched on the padded stool with her hands folded in her lap.

"Isn't he here yet?" she asked, sweetly.

Rosemary eyed her daughter with suspicion. She had *that* look on her face.

"He'll be here any minute," Rosemary said. "Sweetie, you will do as he asks, won't you?"

January was not a *bad* child. She could be naughty, of course – but what child wasn't mischievous occasionally? She was manipulative too when there was something she wanted. And if pressed, Rosemary would admit that whatever January wanted, she usually got. After all, keeping January happy was the important thing.

The current fad was MTV. January had decided that nine years old was the ideal age to become a pop star. She wanted a piano, because Pixie Harmon played piano on MTV, so her parents bought her a baby grand. It cost nearly two thousand pounds, and had to be winched in through the window.

At first things had looked promising. January had donned the little black leather-look top and shorts favoured by Pixie, struck a pose and brought her hands experimentally to the keys. Within an hour Rosemary recognised a stumbling rendition of *Ooh Baby, It's Good*. It was a very simple tune, but it *was* a tune.

January practiced for a week, and each day the tune became a little more fluent, but then her progress halted. She didn't know any other tunes.

To forestall the piano's relegation into the ranks of mere furniture, they had hired a tutor. Having had a series of stern letters from the bank, they'd discovered an obdurate streak in themselves almost as big as their daughter's.

So far there had been five different tutors. For most of them one visit had been enough. Frustrated that natural talent was apparently insufficient, the child refused to be taught. January hid. She screamed and stamped. She played badly on purpose, and stuffed cushions inside the piano lid and pretended it was broken. She even clunked one lady on the head with the metronome.

Now she sat patiently, waiting for tutor number six. She was up to something, but before Rosemary could question her, the doorbell chimed. With one last warning glance, Rosemary went to answer it.

The man standing on her doorstep did not resemble a piano teacher. He was too well dressed. His suit was dark as night and immaculately tailored. His shirt, white as egrets' feathers and stiff as sailcloth under the wind, was bisected by a silk tie that had the exact subtle colouring of the tails of magpies. Rosemary was quite captivated for a moment, until she realised how these wonderful clothes disguised the odd proportions of his body. He had an elongated look, as if stretched like pale toffee. His head flopped on a goosey neck. His beard and moustache were clipped too neatly for his sagging features, as if he'd bought a set of facial hair one size too small for his face. Eyes like dull pennies regarded her blankly. His arms hung down like ropes.

"I'm Linke," he said, in an odd European accent. "I am instructor."

"Thank you for coming," she said, stunned by this apparition on her doorstep. "Please come in." Linke ducked into the hallway behind her.

Outside the music room, a familiar smell assaulted Rosemary's nostrils. A smell that, strangely, reminded her of October. Entering the room she recognised it. It was the smell of the log fire they set when autumn chilled the house.

January was holding the little kitchen blowtorch to the piano. The burnished wood was blackened and blistered, but thus far nothing had actually caught alight. "It won't burn properly," she huffed.

Rosemary was lost for words. But, as she stared at the flames licking the wood, the instructor intervened. Gently, he relieved January of the torch with one skinny hand, and closed her gaping mouth with the other. The child shrank out of the way as he reached over her and rippled an arpeggio on the keyboard.

"Something is wrong," Mr Linke said, and reached into his inside pocket, retrieving a long velvet bag. Inside was a foot-long tuning fork. He struck the fork on the piano to make it hum, a note so low Rosemary could barely hear it, then he handed it to January. The girl immediately dropped it with a squeal.

"The instrument is not well tempered," Linke said. "I shall tune it."

"We've only had the piano a few months," Rosemary protested.

Linke interrupted. "You must leave the room." He laid a fishwhite hand on January's head. "This will stay."

Rosemary disliked Linke's presumption, but she obeyed

nevertheless. Reluctantly, she went into the kitchen and put the kettle on for tea, but as soon as that activity was performed she returned to the music room door. There was no sound from inside: no clinking tools, no twanging strings, no repeated striking of notes. No complaining of child.

Curious, Rosemary peeked through the crack between the door and the jamb. The view was frustratingly limited. January was out of sight, but she caught glimpses of Linke. She couldn't see what he was doing, but he never seemed to linger at the piano. Strangest of all, January remained totally silent.

Consumed by a curiosity that now bordered on concern, Rosemary tried to edge the door open an inch or so to gain a better view. The door was unceremoniously shut in her face. Her level of concern rocketed, and she placed her hand firmly on the handle, determined to interrupt whatever the instructor was doing with her daughter. It was her own door, in her own house, and she had every right to witness the goings on behind that concerned her own child. What stopped her was the first notes of a plodding major scale. Rosemary let a breath out. She had over-reacted, like Richard was always telling her. Plainly, Linke was all right after all.

In the kitchen, the kettle rattled and spat to the boil. As she filled a tray with china, Rosemary heard a melancholy run of notes. Then an entire tune. It was a moody, oddly-intervalled piece. It didn't sound like one of Pixie's songs.

After Linke left, January stayed at the piano, hunched over the keys in concentration. She didn't stop for tea, not even for a chocolate biscuit. Sipping her calming camomile, Rosemary found herself disquieted by the threnodic music, but pleased that her daughter was at least playing the thing, she resisted the growing compulsion to ask January to stop.

Linke did not call again, but in the weeks and months that followed January applied herself to the piano like she never had to anything in her life before. Rosemary and her husband boasted to their friends about their daughter's growing proficiency at the

instrument – they even talked about entering her in a regional competition – but privately both winced when their obedient, silent child came home from school and began to play.

It was some time before Rosemary looked up 'well tempered.' The dictionary didn't tell her much, only that it was a method of tuning keyboard instruments that involved unbalancing the tuning in the common keys by tiny amounts so that they can be tuned in every key.

Rosemary placed the book back into its slot on the shelf, and turned to watch her daughter, hands dancing lightly over the keys of the piano. There was something in that strange music, and in January's cold smile as she concentrated, that brought Rosemary close to weeping.

Harrowfield

When the lawyer left to attend to business in some other part of the building I stood in the doorway of the library at Harrowfield House and beheld a rare treat. It was the archetypal library, the kind immortalised in movies of the nineteen thirties and forties. It occupied two rooms which took up much of one side of the ground floor, high oak shelves stretching along the walls, stout with accumulated knowledge. Subtle lighting picked out the texture of leather, the glint of gold lettering against the sober spectrum presented by the rows of spines. There was a reading table in the centre of the first room, a broad map table in the other.

I breathed in the temple stillness, a hush that was one part anticipation and one part respect, and savoured the prospect of what would be my retreat and my work for the next two or three days.

Then a phone began to warble. It was my damned mobile. Communications technology is the curse of the modern age. That anyone thought it was desirable to be able to be contacted anywhere, any time, no matter how inopportune the moment is beyond me. However, Christine had worn me down with common sense, persuading me to buy one for keeping in touch when I was out – as she put it – on my travels. I could not deny that it made sense, in terms of our business at least, but I didn't have to like it.

I stabbed the answer key.

"Charlie-*boy*. Where are you?"

I hadn't heard the voice for two years, but it was as familiar to me as my old rugby injury.

Massimo Grieve.

My dreams of solitude evaporated.

Fifteen years earlier Grieve and I had shared university digs up in Glasgow. We hadn't got on, though we had managed to co-exist, the way flatmates must, with a minimum of interaction. Perversely, while contact with my friends withered over the years, Grieve had stayed with me. A recurring disruptive force in my life. Possibly he mellowed, or perhaps it was enforced habit that eventually made us friends. Friends of sorts anyway. Our last encounter had been fractious.

"I'm up in the Lakes," I said. "A place called Harrowfield. They asked me up to catalogue…"

"The Douglas Randall place? He's dead is he? Excellent. Listen, Charlie, I'm in Manchester right now so I can be with you after lunch sometime. See you about two? Good. We can catch up then."

The line went dead. Whatever the call had originally been about I would possibly never know, but the mention of Harrowfield had caught his interest. I felt a lump of anticipation settle in my stomach. My first thought had been that Grieve's call was nothing more than coincidence. But coincidences followed him like scavenging crows.

Three things always come to mind about Grieve from the student days: the kind of brain that guaranteed him his first class degree while allowing him to pursue a lifestyle of dope and daytime

128

TV, an infantile fascination with 'True Crime' books and the pages of *Fortean Times*, and the fact that any encounter with him always left you with more questions than answers. Questions like: what was his interest in Douglas Randall; and how the hell did he get the number of my new phone?

I was eating a pre-packed sandwich in my car when Grieve arrived. A cold drizzle had begun to streak the windscreen as I chewed and watched the wind toss gulls about over the little lake and its bleak shores. Choppy waves lapped almost up to the walls of the house.

The morning had gone well. An initial inspection had revealed that the library contained a selection of biographies and fiction, small in number but sporting a few intriguing items. Reference books and histories took up the remainder of the shelf space in the first room, but it was the second room that interested me most. As I had expected, the Randall family had assembled one of the most extensive collections of maritime histories and nautical charts in the country. It would fetch a fair amount at auction.

Grieve had changed his car again. This time it was a sleek, Japanese affair, deep metallic blue. The top was down, allowing the rain in and, unfortunately, letting out the jaunty blare of what sounded like a Tijuana Brass rendition of *Spanish Flea*.

The car and music stopped and the roof rolled up smoothly. Grieve got out and stood appraising the house. A leather coat fluttered tent-like about his wide frame, the wind riffling through his springy thundercloud of dark hair. The sideburns if anything were even bushier than last time I'd seen him, and the sunglasses were his customary affectation. He carried a slim metallic case. Perhaps all this was what passed for acceptable dress in the computer consultancy business these days, or perhaps it was just Grieve being an insufferable poser as usual.

I got out to meet him, slightly conscious of the conservative cut of my own Slater Bros suit.

"Impressive, isn't it?" I said.

"I suppose so." Grieve fixed his attention on the house. It loomed – an impassive façade of grey sandstone and glass, peaked and turreted on the top like some combination of chalet and keep. "If by impressive you mean *big*," he muttered sarcastically.

This was another Grieve thing. Never one for bothering with hellos and goodbyes, he suddenly appeared in your life and carried on where he had left off. He'd been here no more than a few minutes and already my back was up.

"Grieve, why are you here?" I asked.

He looked surprised. I wasn't always so forthright. "Same reason as you, Charlie. Books." He laid a patronising hand on my arm. "You know the kind I mean," he went on. "It's been more or less common knowledge that Randall was a dabbler, and rumour has it that over the years he acquired some very rare volumes of an occult nature. It's that old classic pattern: bereavement to spiritualism to dabblings on the dark side."

Glib as it was, this matched pretty closely what the lawyer had told me. Randall had inherited the house and a world wide shipping business on his father's death in 1948. He had come home to England in the autumn of that year, leaving his young American wife to follow, but she had died before she could join him. Perhaps not too surprisingly, grief-stricken, Randall had become a recluse, especially in the fifteen years since his retirement. Anything beyond those facts of course was total fantasy of the pulpiest kind, the stuff of those hammy seventies horror movies, and just the sort of thing Grieve would go for. The 'rumour' he spoke of could likely be traced to the kind of conjecture that was rife in those post-war years when spiritualism was at its peak.

So that was why he was here. Magick books. I was a little disappointed but not surprised. Grieve's fascination with the occult went back as long as I'd known him. He loved mystery. He aspired to it and he sought it out wherever he suspected two and two could spookily be added to make five. The last time he'd dropped in on me he had been looking for a book of reproductions of the sketches made by the hermit, William Rae. In the twenties Rae had been discovered living in isolation in Sutherland in Northern Scotland. His cabin had been littered with renditions of his, by all accounts very disturbing, dreams, and the pictures were supposed to have been collected into a volume, now much sought after. Of course my contacts had been unable to locate any trace of it and I doubted it had ever existed. In my experience that was how these things usually turned out.

"You know, Charlie," Grieve said, "there are people who would be very interested in preventing these books going to public auction."

"That would be a matter for the estate. Not me," I said, unhappy at the insinuated slur on my professional integrity. Whether these *people* meant himself or someone he was acting for I didn't care to know.

"I understand," he said, "but I'm confident an arrangement can be made."

"Whatever," I allowed myself a smirk at his confidence. "But I haven't seen anything remotely occult yet, I'm afraid."

"Trust me," Grieve said. "They're here." He named some titles. I recognised two. These were not books in general circulation and I doubted there was even one copy of either in the country.

"Well, if you say so, I'm sure we'll find them," I sighed. Getting rid of Grieve could be difficult. Asking him straight out to leave would make him more determined to stay. If he had nothing better to do, I decided, he could hang around until the work was done and he was satisfied that his information was wrong. Following him inside I added, "If by *occult* you mean shipping records."

*

"What's missing from this picture?" Grieve's voice surprised me. I had become so absorbed in my work that I'd almost managed to forget his presence. Entering the library's nautical room I found

131

him bending over the table, reading lamps illuminating the heap of maps strewn across it. I held my annoyance and looked over his shoulder.

He tapped the uppermost map with a forefinger. The chart was a black and white, laminated affair showing the physical geography of a southern part of the Lake District. Dense finger-print whorls represented the profusion of peaks. Towards the foot of the map I recognised a pattern of hills, the way the road snaked down and then curled around, and there, marked by name, was the house.

I shook my head. "What are you on about, Grieve?"

He shot me a look, a little smile. Then he flipped the map up and revealed a modern colour OS map of more or less the same area.

I still didn't see. I said so.

He laid down the first map again and lifted it. Laid it, lifted it. Eventually he said, "The Lake!"

He was right. The older rendering omitted the lake outside the house.

"Nineteen forty seven," he said, pointing. Then the newer map, "Nineteen seventy."

"You're saying the lake suddenly appeared on the map sometime between forty seven and seventy," I said, feeling as stupid as I sounded.

"I don't think geology works that fast," he said pointedly.

I shrugged. I wasn't sure he was right, but decided to let it ride. Sure enough though, on the earlier map the area at the side of the house currently occupied by the lake was clearly marked as an area of open land. *Harrow Field.*

"Cartographical error?" I ventured.

He produced two more maps, slapping them down a little dramatically. "Not unless they missed it in thirty one and oh-nine as well."

"Perhaps they just copied the old maps and repeated an old error," I suggested. I realised that he was trying to imply something

– God knew what – mysterious in all this and I was suddenly determined not to encourage him with it, adding, "or maybe it was a natural disaster?"

He frowned at me then grinned. "Who knows? Shouldn't be too hard to find out though, should it?"

*

When Grieve returned about forty minutes later I tried to ignore him, but was peripherally aware of him inspecting the shelves in a casual, almost bored, fashion. He didn't mention the lake.

"So where do you reckon the magic books are," he said.

I paused in my note-taking, pen poised above the ledger. "Have you tried under M?"

"Very funny."

"Well how about that old favourite, the secret room? That's the traditional place for a forbidden library, isn't it?" I looked over to see a grin illuminating his face, like that of a child that has just tricked an adult into giving him his own way. He seemed to take my suggestion, flippant as it was, as permission to probe around the shelves and began to pull books out at random.

My concentration broken, I watched this performance for a full minute before my patience ran out. "So what about the lake?" I said.

Grieve stopped what he was doing. His impish smile confirmed that he'd been waiting for me to ask.

"It's just a lake," he said. "Except that it appears to have no tributaries." He returned to the reading table and sat down, spreading his hands flat in front of him and stretching his legs underneath. "Oh," he added, "and it's salt water. Aha!"

There was a click followed by a smooth rumbling noise. To my astonishment a square section rose out of the centre of the table. The section was shelved and had the capacity to hold a number of large volumes, but the shelves were empty.

Grieve ran a finger along a shelf, looked thoughtful. "No dust," he said.

"Bravo, Grieve." I laughed. "You've discovered a forbidden library with no books."

Then I stopped laughing as I was suddenly gripped by the conviction that someone else had entered the room. But when I turned I found the doorway empty.

"Charlie?" I heard Grieve say behind me.

Ignoring him, I stepped out into the hall. It was empty too, but there was something unusual. A smell. Fresh, with a sharp tang to it, familiar but out of place against the waxy odour of the house.

"Mrs Caldwell?" I called, thinking it had been the lawyer I had sensed, but she did not reply. The light in the hall had a sullen quality, filtering through the frosted panels around the front door to cast a moiré pattern the colour of beaten copper on the polished wooden floor. I was reminded of the sea at sunset. Then a shadow passed across the glass and the sound of the doorbell made me jump.

Since the bell still did not immediately bring the lawyer, I opened the door myself. Two men stood there in identical blue overalls. The digging tools in the truck parked behind them completed the picture. I led them around the house to the little chapel perched up the hillside. The family plot lay behind it. There was now a biting edge to the breeze coming off the lake, heavy cloud having gathered during the course of the afternoon. The chapel doors were ajar and we found Caldwell inside. While she took the diggers off to the grave site I lingered, intent on a moment more's respite from the wind. A deep chill had settled inside me.

The chapel was a sombre affair, solidly constructed from grey sandstone. Isolated electric lights shed a little warm illumination which only emphasised the shadows. The building was barely large enough for three narrow ranks of pews and the open coffin at the front. From my vantage at the door I could see little of the contents – a supine form in a black suit, pale face at the top, white gloves clasped at waist level.

"Douglas Randall, I presume," said Grieve mordantly as he pushed past me for a better look. I hovered by the door. "Funny how you can tell they were rich even when they're dead," he said. "The gloves are a bit much though. Makes him look like a snooker referee on a rest break. When did he die?"

"Saturday," replied the lawyer, re-entering the chapel having discharged instructions to the diggers. "The family was notified, but is spread pretty far afield, I'm afraid. There are cousins and such in the USA and New Zealand. None, that we could trace here in the UK, however. It'll be a quick interment tomorrow if there are no mourners."

"How did he die?" said Grieve.

Caldwell peered at him, as if registering him for the first time. "I'm sorry, but who are you?"

Feeling stupid for not having introduced him immediately, I did so now. It was no more than a vague introduction but Caldwell seemed to accept it. She nodded, pushed a stray strand of greying, blonde hair away from her pinched face.

"Mr Randall fell down the stairs – the coroner believed on his way to bed. He was on a course of medication for his heart," she said unhelpfully. "Now gentlemen, it's getting late. If it's okay with you I have to get back to the office, so I'll have to ask you to pack up for the night." She looked as if she was glad to be leaving. I couldn't say why, but at that moment I felt exactly the same way.

*

I had a room in the village hotel. It came as no surprise to find that Grieve had discovered this and booked himself into the same place. We ate in the little dining room. Half a dozen tables squeezed into disturbingly floral surroundings. The food was bland, but hot and filling, and I felt the inner chill recede at last.

While Grieve ordered coffees, I excused myself. On my return I discovered that the few other diners had departed and that Grieve had opened up his silver case on our cleared table. Inside the case was the smallest, meanest looking laptop computer I'd ever seen. A loose black coil connected it to his mobile phone. Grieve was tapping delicately at the keyboard.

"Just doing a wee search on Randall," he said as I sat down. "Obits from the *New York Times* in the late forties came up with something interesting."

The waitress arrived with a stainless steel pot, steam curling from the spout. She tried to find a space on the table but gave up and set it on the adjoining table along with the milk jug and bowl of sugar sachets. When she was gone I slipped around to see what Grieve had found. The uppermost of the windows on the screen contained a transcript of a 1949 *New York Times* obituary which reported that Jayne Randall had died on January 22nd when the passenger ship, *Galatea*, part of the Randall Empire line, had sunk in the North Atlantic. One hundred and seventy two others had drowned that day. This was followed by a report of the extravagant memorial service, a picture of a long line of black cars.

"Well," said Grieve, "that perhaps explains why there are no direct heirs – but it does add to the mystery, doesn't it?"

"What mystery?" I was immediately irritated. "Grieve, there is no *mystery* here. Randall is just a dead old man with a tragedy in his past. Leave it at that."

Of course, he couldn't. He waited me out with that knowing expression until I had to try again.

"He lost her fifty years ago," I said. "How do you know he didn't marry again? Or take a mistress."

"The only beneficiaries were distant cousins. Your Mrs Caldwell told us that," Grieve stressed with laboured patience. "Since he was a widower there was no reason to prevent him marrying another lover. Even if he hadn't married again, the mistress and any kids would surely have been named in the will."

"So, he didn't marry again," I said.

"Exactly," Grieve replied.

"It's not exactly a mystery."

"On its own, no. But then there's the lake."

"Oh give it up, Grieve." I felt my voice tense in annoyance.

He looked at me levelly, then asked, "What did you see – back there in the library?"

The switch of subject confused me for a moment. I'd almost forgotten. "Nothing," I said.

Grieve raised an eyebrow.

"Really," I insisted. "I saw nothing. It was just a feeling, an impression that someone was standing in the doorway. A woman…"

"You saw a woman?"

"No. I told you. There was no-one there. It was just a feeling, that's all. I thought it was Mrs Caldwell." Grieve was paying close attention and I was acutely uncomfortable with the direction of his train of thought. "It was just my imagination," I said. "What else could it have been?"

Whatever reply he may have had for that question was derailed by the irritating cartoon melody of my mobile. It was Christine. She told me that the new shipment of stock for our antiquarian bookshop had at last arrived from Holland. One of the bibles had been sold, but apart from that trade was slow. Nothing new. Business news updated, there was a pause, a heartbeat which I was not inclined at that moment to fill. Then she rang off cheerfully. Guiltily I suppressed a wish that she hadn't phoned.

"Married?" Grieve asked as I pocketed the phone. I nodded, suddenly feeling as if I'd scored a secret point in the game for managing to keep information from the man who knew everything.

"How's it going?" he said.

"Fine," I said. Then added, "great."

Grieve nodded. I didn't know whether in acceptance of

137

what I said or in confirmation of some hidden thought of his own.

*

Sleep came uneasily. The room was unbelievably small and the radiators appeared to be stuck at their highest setting. I lay tossing my thoughts around in the dark and realised that I had been on edge since arriving at Harrowfield. I wanted to put it down to Grieve's usual unsettling effect on me but it felt like there was more to it than that. I pushed Grieve from my mind, and thought instead about Christine. I wondered if she was asleep yet, or lying awake like me. I tried to picture her face. I tried very hard.

When I did manage to drop off it was with the help of the hypnotic rattle of the rain against the window.

I dreamt of rain too. It was raining inside the room, water falling silently through a wedge of sodium light from the street. I could see the distinct drops clearly, and as they passed through the amber light they slowed, descending like glittering beads on threads. Then a hand appeared. The fingers were slender, the wrist fine and articulate, and where the hand intersected the light I could see that it consisted of sparkling, fizzing vapour. A hand made of bright rain.

It reached towards me and where it touched my chest I felt such a shocking cold that I woke at once. I was not surprised to find the sheets damp, my body drenched. As I became properly awake I realised that this, and the faint tang of salt I still detected in the air, were due to a sweaty night in a hot room, and nothing more.

*

I felt a churlish pleasure that Grieve did not appear at breakfast. This ill slept, I really wasn't in the mood for him. I half hoped he'd given up and gone home, so my humour worsened when I drove to the house to find his car there before mine. The sky was bruised with ugly clouds and the wind was cold, bullying me across the drive towards the front door. Grieve's voice stopped me.

"Charlie!"

I couldn't see him at first, but when he called again I spotted him, absurdly hanging out of a second floor window along the side of the house that faced over the lake. I walked around.

"What the hell are you doing?" I shouted, not disguising my disapproval.

"Look." He seemed excitable, good-naturedly ignoring my own mood. He was wedged half out of the left-most of three identical windows. With a struggle he extricated himself and vanished. I waited and, feeling the edge of the wind at my back, pulled my collar up and stepped into the lea of the house. My feet were suddenly cold too. Looking down I discovered that I was standing in a puddle around an overflowing drain. Cursing, I stepped back. The drainpipe spewed dirty looking water. I followed it up and saw that it exited the house below the middle of the three windows. Grieve reappeared at the right hand of these.

"There's no door," he shouted gleefully, then, seeing that I wasn't following him, "come up and I'll show you."

I didn't believe him at first, but eventually he proved to me that whatever room the middle window belonged to had no door – at least not one that we could find. There were two doors on the east second floor landing. Both opened onto rather non-descript guest bedrooms: bare, functional rooms that, although clean enough, had a look of disuse about them. Considering Randall's reclusive tendencies, this was hardly surprising.

Rather desperately I suggested that the window between the two rooms may have been purely decorative, that there was no third room. A certain amount of unproductive tapping and listening at walls hinted otherwise but an inspection of the dimensions of the bedrooms suggested that any room that might exist would have to be pretty narrow. I couldn't imagine that anyone would build such a room. Grieve though was convinced.

"So where is it, Charlie?" he exclaimed. "Where's the door?"

I shrugged. A flurry of rain pattered against the window, spattering the windowsill, and I pulled the sash down. It was sticky, requiring some effort before it closed with a thump.

"Grieve, it's an old house," I said, and a solution suggested itself. "One large room got knocked into two and instead of splitting a window they built either side of it. Simple explanation. End of story. I'm going to get back to my work."

I meant it. Whatever mystery his brain was concocting to tie together these otherwise unnoteworthy elements was an attempt to justify his belief that Randall had a secret collection, and it existed purely in Grieve's imagination. Randall had been no more than a tragic widower, the lake a curious natural phenomenon, and the supposed library had never existed. I'd had enough. The morning was wearing on and there was a lot to be done before the lawyer returned at five. It appeared that she'd stuck only long enough for one of us to arrive. It seemed she didn't care to spend much time at Harrowfield House.

I left the room and was about to descend the stair when my body was seized by a cramp of cold. I clutched the banister for a few seconds and then the spasms of painful shivers left me as suddenly as they had come. It felt as though whatever had gripped me had flown from me, rushed out of my chest and my extremities to the other end of the landing. Looking in that direction, I saw that there was another flight at the far end, leading upwards and ending at a single door. Since the second floor was nominally the top of the house, I guessed the door led to an attic space.

"Grieve," I said, climbing the stairs. "Look at this." I stopped short of the door. My heart clenched. The air up this one flight of stairs was noticeably colder; it smelled fresh, tainted with a saline edge. I laid my hand on the brass door handle and snatched it back. "Jesus!"

"Cold?" Grieve said.

I nodded. I could see now that what I had taken to be a film of dust on the handle was in fact a rime of frost.

Grieve moved past me. His shoes squelched. Along the bottom of the door the carpet was soaked. He crouched, sank his fingers into the weave and then lifted them to his nose, sniffed them, licked them. "Salt water," he said. Then turning to me, "Like the hall yesterday?"

That was the smell. Salt water. My mind raced for an explanation that did not involve whatever Grieve was thinking right now. Anything that wasn't mysterious. Supernatural. I couldn't think of one. The words slipped out, "And I had a dream last night."

He stood and wiped his hand on his trousers. In the face of his expectation I briefly described my dream. Grieve subjected me to a look of appraisal which I could not easily interpret, but in parts it bore resemblance to comprehension, suspicion and envy. Then he stepped past me and used the cuff of his coat to turn the handle.

The door opened onto darkness. Grieve reached into his coat and pulled out a penlight. He flicked it on. "It's a boy scout thing," he said, stepping through the doorway.

Even as I followed him I wondered what the hell I was doing. This was not a rational activity for two adults to be pursuing in a dead man's house – but the salty air prickling my skin and the sudden deep cold returning to fill my bones were not rational either. I allowed myself to be led.

Under the sweep of Grieve's narrow beam we could see that the attic was only partially floored. Narrow walkways of planking led around the outer construction of the stairwell and stretched into the darkness. Between them lay exposed beams. We would have to watch where we put our feet unless we were in a particular hurry to go downstairs. Grieve set off around the stairwell. I followed, feeling the rough brickwork with my right hand. He played his light around. Searching. In the quick illumination I made out the shapes of lumber – trunks and suitcases, grey with stoor and less identifiable, curiously humped forms under sheets. Somewhere, water dripped in a tank.

"There," Grieve said at length.

I followed the beam of the torch. A short distance away under the slope of the roof lay a metallic structure. An extendable ladder. We followed the walkway in that direction, and where I had been expecting to have to step between the joists found that a couple of loose planks had been laid directly to the ladder. I guessed as soon as I saw the ladder that there would be a trap door leading down into the third room. A padlock lay in the dust between the beams. Grieve lifted the door and a cold blast of wet air swept up into the attic. The ladder appeared to have been there for years, yet it slid easily as we lowered it into the room. Grieve almost knocked me out of the way to get down first.

"Oh, God," I heard Grieve say as I followed him. My foot grew cold as it contacted the floor with a soft slopping sound. For the second time that day I was standing in an inch of grey water.

If previously I had been reluctant to consider anything unusual at Harrowfield House I could not deny it now. At the very least, Douglas Randall had been out of his mind.

From where I stood to the window at the far end, the room was about twenty five feet in length but could have been no more than six feet wide. The floor and walls and ceiling had been coated and sealed with some clear brown substance. Gutters ran along the sides.

There could be no other explanation for this than the room had been designed to hold water.

Then I saw the reason for Grieve's anguish, and I shared it. There were books half submerged in the water, pages floating loose. He handed them up to me. They were ugly books, thickly bound and heavy with moisture. Among the titles were those Grieve had mentioned earlier. I had never expected, nor indeed wanted, to come across volumes of this rarity. In my trade, there are certain kinds of books it is best not to pursue. These would have been worth as much as the rest of the collection to the right buyers, but seeing how warped they were, I knew without trying to prise apart the pages that Randall's occult library was ruined. I stacked the books on a rough shelf that had been screwed inexpertly to the wall. It was landscaped with laval sculptures of melted red wax.

"What went on in here?" I said, astonished by the room. "And where is the water coming from?"

Grieve stood, in his hands one last book, slimmer than the rest, and a box of lacquered black wood. As he stepped aside I saw the window properly for the first time. It was a plain sash window. Four panes of dirty glass, each with a dark fringe of mildew. Outside the skies had cleared some and the rain had abated. Which made it all the more difficult to explain the water pooling on the sill, streaming down the wall feeding the drain in the floor beneath the window. Mentally I connected it with the drainpipe outside.

"It must be leaking down from the roof. Perhaps the guttering is blocked," I said, not really believing what I was saying, but unable to come up with a credible alternative. I pushed down on the sash to try and close it but the frame was obviously too warped for it to budge.

Grieve had been examining the slim book. "No," he said quietly and handed it to me. It was a simple note book: no identifying marks on the stained cover, no names or dates on the inside, only a mess of gluey pages smeared with washed out ink. Peeling them apart, however, I discovered that not all of the writing – and I was certain it was Randall's – had been rendered unreadable. A few pages were just about legible, although I soon realised that legibility did not guarantee comprehension.

"*Making the wards has exhausted me,*" I read aloud. "*I could sleep for a hundred days but at last I am ready. I won't be delayed. I know I should not do this, but I cannot* not *do it. God*

143

help me." Grieve met my incredulity with a flat expression, indicating that I should continue. On the next page, *"Oh, dear God, it worked. But we had so little time. So little time."*

The next clump of pages was so sodden that they ripped pulpily when I tried to separate them. Then I came across this: *"It is over. I lost control and almost lost everything, least of which my life. I panicked. So much water. How will I explain the lake?"* After this, underlined, *"It is over."*

There was not much more, only one passage, near the end. *"The wards are almost gone. I don't think I have the strength to make more. I will see her just once more, and then, God willing…"*

After that the pages were blank.

There was no doubt now that Grieve was right.

"What are 'wards'?" I asked.

"Objects that allow the user to control power," Grieve said. "In this case I imagine they allowed Randall to open a portal – to somewhere pretty wet by the looks of it."

"A portal?" I breathed, shocked at myself that I could lend the idea any credence. "A portal to where?"

He indicated the steady stream from the window. "Looks like he wasn't able to close it properly the last time. Perhaps for some reason he had to leave before he was finished. That might even have been what killed him." His face lit up as the logic of it unfolded, filling in the blanks in his understanding of events. "Yes! He became ill. That's why the trap door wasn't locked and why the books weren't returned to the library." Grieve's eyes were bright with the adventure. He was having the time of his life. "But what did Randall mean by 'God willing'? And he must have known the spells he needed to make the wards by heart, so why did he tote his whole library up here? Charlie, I think he was trying something new. I wonder what he was up to."

"To *where*, Grieve?" I had begun to shiver again, and not just from the cold.

Before he could answer, the window rattled violently in its frame, raising an inch, and the water began to pour into the room. It gushed over the sill, became a curtain falling to the floor and sent waves the length of the room. Crying out, I managed to keep my feet as it sloshed around my ankles, soaking my trousers with icy wash, but Grieve reeled back a couple of steps, falling on his knees. The wave broke weakly against the far wall sending ripples down the gutters.

Then a figure rose from the water. Not from underneath the surface, but out of it. By its shape a woman, water coursing down from her brow, around the line of her chin, pouring across her narrow shoulders, the subtle curves of her breasts and hips, feeding the cascade that was her legs before merging with the surface water in a swirl of currents.

A woman made of water. None of her features was defined, only hinted at – a pair of swirling eddies billowed loose sand where the eyes would be, a clot of weed tumbling in the place that marked the mouth. Impossible as it was, I knew her – except where in my dream she had been made of rain, now she was composed of darker, murkier water. I could not escape the impression from her stance and the inclination of her head that she recognised me also.

Then she spoke and her voice was the brittle cry of gulls, the creaking of sea ice in the cold, dead water far from land. "Douglas?" she said. She was asking me. I think Grieve sensed this and, although it must have killed him to be excluded, was unwilling to do anything that might break the spell. Regaining his feet, he said nothing but his eyes widened, signalling that I should answer.

I knew who she was – could only be. Jayne, Douglas Randall's wife. Blocking the train of impossibilities that assumption engendered, I said, "I'm sorry, your husband is dead."

Possibly she had guessed this already. Her head bowed. A spear of sullen light broke through the clouds outside, falling diagonally across her torso, illuminating the dark water of her core. The only sound in the room was the constant streaming of water.

An impact behind us broke the moment. The window creaked alarmingly and the sash shot up a clear foot as water surged into the room. Through the open gap I was amazed to see an expanse of grey sea. Ugly waves rolled high, crashed down in unrelenting rhythm. I could not reconcile the otherwise normal view of cloudy weather seen through the top half of the window with this angry seascape through the bottom. As if to convince me that this was not some kind of illusion, a gust of freezing sea air assaulted us.

Then in the troughs I saw heads appear. First one, then another, then as if some rumour was spreading beneath the waves, they became a crowd. The heads rode the swells, disappeared in the troughs, reappeared. They were of the same manner of being as the woman that stood beside us – and they were coming closer to the window. Beneath the crashing of the deep water their voices rose in furious anguish.

In answer, the apparition that had been Jayne Randall let out a god-awful shriek. It spurred us both into reaction.

"Oh, Jesus," Grieve shouted, sloshing towards me. We reached for the window together and threw all our weight into forcing it down. It was stuck fast.

"The ward."

It was Randall's wife. In an outstretched hand she held the box. Grieve had dropped it when he fell. As he stepped towards her to take it the next wave hit him squarely in the back and he pitched forward, through the water woman and disappeared momentarily under the surface. That wave was followed immediately by another surge. I gripped the side of the window, resisting the flow, but Grieve was swept to the end of the room, colliding with the ladder.

In those two gulping surges the water had risen above my waist. The people in the sea were approaching disturbingly fast, their voices carrying on the bitter wind that froze my fingers, turned my trousers into an icy second skin. They were now close enough to make out faces, etched with expressions of loss and recrimination. Then they disappeared beneath the waves, reappeared once more. Closer.

I thought Mrs Randall had vanished as well. Then she rose in front of me. Box in hand.

I took it. It was a simple little thing, decorated with some oriental pattern, black layered on black. A twist of the saline encrusted lug released the lid. Inside was a parcel of folded velvet, and nestling within the sodden material, I found a ring of cloudy metal. Surprisingly it was warm to touch and when I held it up to the light I saw that it was not metal, but glass. A torus of glass etched with an inscription too faint to read, and inside the glass what looked like captive smoke, coiling sinuously. It was beautiful.

"Put it on," the woman implored.

I almost dropped it as the next wave caught me by surprise, sending me down. Numb cold enveloped my head, as the current swept me away from the window. When I resurfaced the water level had risen still further. I struggled back towards the window.

Instinct made me slip the ring on to my wedding finger. Smoky glass and plain simple gold gleamed in the turbulent light from the absurdly disconnected Lake District sky through the top half of the window. The ward's warmth against my skin was comforting.

I heaved down on the sash. Nothing. It was as stuck as before. The window vibrated as something jostled it from the other side.

"Break it," the woman pleaded. "Don't let them into my house."

I didn't understand.

"Charlie," Grieve said, leaning unsteadily on the ladder, "it's a closing rite. You'll have to destroy the ward to close the portal." He coughed, belching water. "But don't do it."

I stared at him in disbelief. I was terrified of what even now was closing on this room. I wanted nothing more than to have that window safely shut.

"There's nothing to be scared of," he said. "They're no more dangerous than she is."

"How can you know that?" I gasped.

Grieve grinned sourly. "I think I got a stomachful of her when I took that last tumble." I couldn't tell if he was being serious. "Charlie, she's manipulating us – you. When Randall didn't return to complete what he started that last time, she led you here to do it. To close the portal and bring her home from the loneliness of the sea. But what about the others? Don't they deserve the same chance?"

The water woman hissed like steam, then erupted in a jet of spray that hit him square in the chest, sending him under once more.

Behind me the window rattled against the onslaught of the sea. Through the open window I saw the passengers and crew of the *Galatea*, clustered on the other side of the sill. Their faces bore such pain, such fury, such hope that I froze. For a moment Grieve's argument stayed my desperation to shut them out. The ward buzzed warmly around my finger. I clenched it in a protective fist. With this power, why should I not try to save what remained of these souls? Then the water became a turbulent cloud as the mass of them rushed for the gap. In panic I brought my fist down on the sill and, despite the drag of the water, managed to summon sufficient force to smash the ring. The water boiled around my hand and scalding pain seared through my finger. At the same time, energy drained out of me, down my arm and through my blistering hand. The window crashed shut.

*

The drainpipe overflow had created a direct channel to the lake. It was still flowing. We passed it on the way up to the chapel.

Grieve said he wanted to pay his last respects, but I knew he wanted the last piece of evidence, the proof that he'd figured everything out correctly. This was a couple of hours after I'd let him haul me out of the room and treat my hand while both we and our clothes dried off in the kitchen. He didn't mention that amid the blisters he had seen the ring of raw letters branded into my flesh.

As soon as I was bandaged up he announced his intention to leave. I thought his haste a little off, but couldn't really blame him. He had what he came for after all. The books from Randall's secret room, ruined as they were, sat in the boot of his car. I didn't begrudge him them, and to be truthful I was happier not having to include them in the catalogue and explain the state they were in.

Inside the chapel Grieve said, "Well? Shall we have a look?" He approached the coffin and lifted Randall's hand. Gently he tugged off the glove.

The fingers looked whittled. Crossed and crossed again with old scars. The pain of making the portal was written all over them in tiny scratchy letters.

Fifty years. I imagined the lonely evenings when he would weaken and summon her out of the sea. I imagined them in that room. Each occasion special but inadequate, sharing words because they could share nothing else. The agony as he sent her away.

"Do you think she went back," I said as we retraced our steps. "When we closed the window."

"No," Grieve answered. "I think Randall realised he was too old to go on making the wards, so he went for broke and tried to bring her through permanently, or at least for an extended duration. But it cost him too much. He couldn't close the portal afterwards, probably died trying to reach his pills. It almost worked, though. Now Jayne was rooted here and with Randall gone she had to find a way to close the portal. She chose you."

"You think she knew he was dead?"

Grieve nodded. "I think so. If not for certain, then she had a pretty firm suspicion when he left things undone."

"Then why did she want to be here so badly? What difference did it make?"

Grieve looked at me strangely. "Love? Remembrance? I don't know. I'd have thought you'd know more about those things than me. I don't suppose it's surprising that she'd choose to be here to remember him alone. Beats the crowded North Atlantic anyway. Selfish bitch."

While I felt a welling of guilt about consigning the people of the *Galatea* to the bitter monotony of the place where they had died, I thought Grieve's cynicism a little damning. I wondered if he had seen the chapel floor. A pool of salt water like fifty years worth of tears.

As he was getting into his car, Grieve treated me to one of those looks. Eventually he said, "You're lucky, you know that?"

I raised a hand to the back of the speeding vehicle, and then Grieve was gone.

Gulls argued noisily over the lake and its salt-spoiled shores. Whatever was left behind of Jayne Randall – whatever eroded, polished vestige of dead love – she had what she wanted. Harrowfield was a drowned place. She was welcome to it.

Grieve's parting remark snagged in my thoughts. At first I thought he had been referring jealously to my interaction with Jayne Randall's – I suppose he would call it – 'spirit'. But that was being more than a little uncharitable. Perhaps he meant something else entirely.

I fished my mobile out of my pocket, dialled carefully.

"Christine?" I said. "It's me. No, nothing's wrong. I just wanted to talk."

The Apparatus

Let me tell you about ghosts. I don't believe in them. In my youth I saw too much fakery where the spirit world was concerned to have any doubts. Even if I choose the supernatural explanation of what we saw that last time, and take as more than coincidence what followed, I still require further evidence. And no matter how hard I have prayed for it over the years since, it has never come.

Séances, in those days, were the talk of the steamie, and Glasgow had a level of spiritualist activity approaching a small industry. It had been three years since the end of the Great War, and the nexts of kin were still groping around in a sort of muddled communal grief for a clue, a hint, an inkling to the whereabouts of all those husbands and fathers and sons who had disappeared in the muddy fields of Europe, turning to whatever means they could find to provide them with something approaching closure. The ones who came back were little use, cold and iron-faced men who preferred to batter their frustrations like bullets into the rivet

151

holes of the great ships or scribble their memories on plate steel in hot, unreadable welds. The kirk offered comfort only for those who knew for certain the fate of their men. So, it was to the spiritualist churches, the travelling mediums on their borough hall tours, and the furtive parlour séances that many turned in search of their ghosts.

My sister was one such lost soul. Her husband, John, was one of the thousands who simply never returned from the Somme, and in the inconclusive limbo that followed, while the rest of the country picked itself up and went forward, Margaret developed an unhealthy addiction to séance meetings. To begin with I attended a few of these evenings. They were entertaining enough in their own way, but the novelty quickly wore off. I don't know which I found more distasteful: the obvious parlour tricks employed by the various practitioners she invited to the house on Partick Hill, or the sincerity with which she and her cronies professed to believe it all. That they were truly able to converse with their lost ones in the spirit world. A frustratingly vague practice it was, a fog of mystery threaded through with just enough teases and glimpses to feed the needy audience. It was easy to see how the table-knockers and conjurers kept the repeat business coming.

It was no coincidence that I began visiting my sister less often around the time I fell in love with Helen. Helen was the perfect antidote to the post-war depression. She was bright and beautiful, and filled with an optimism for the future that, if others could not quite see yet what she founded it on, they could still not help but be infected by it. By comparison, Margaret's stubborn adherence to the past was dispiriting to say the least.

As it happened, the day we visited her to announce our engagement, she was having yet another of her séances.

"You will stay?" Her face was pale enough against her sombre dress that it occurred to me that her obsession with the spirit world was drawing her nearer to the wraiths than them to her. "This Mr Gilfillan has a new technique that is said to work wonders."

I was disappointed, and perhaps a little angry, that she chose to indulge her obsession rather than help us celebrate our good news. I was of a mind to curtail our visit, but Helen's eyes brightened at the mention of a séance.

"Oh, please, Bert," she said. "I've always wanted to try this. Please, let's stay."

It was difficult to tell whether Margaret found such vibrant enthusiasm appropriate, but I could see that it was important to her to have me there. After all, I was the only other person that had known John well enough to be able to corroborate his appearance, should such a miracle transpire.

So it was that an hour later we found ourselves sitting around the dining room table. The other guests that had arrived in the interim, Margaret's hard core séance circle, perched among us like a flock of dapper crows, each with a thimble of fino and a funereal air that made me want to scream.

The odd assembly was completed by the figure at the far end of the table. In the unhealthy glow of the low-turned gas lamps, he looked to me like nothing more than a door-stepping tinker. His worsted wool suit may have been his best, but I had observed a flap of unstitched lining, a button dangling on its thread. Not for this Gilfillan the velvet cape or the crass soubriquet. He was not *that* kind of charlatan at least. Nor had he come with the usual bag of tricks employed by his contemporaries to enliven the business of talking to the dead. No, he sat there, ruddy faced and irritable, like a man wondering where his next pint was coming from.

Despite myself, I admit I was intrigued. In addition to Gilfillan my attention was also taken by the bulky, velvet-draped object that sat in the centre of the table, and I knew that this was not going to be the usual cut-rate *son et lumiere*.

"Good afternoon," the man said in a slovenly, antipodean drawl. "I sense that many of you have sought communion with

153

the spirit before, and who knows, perhaps a few of you have made some sort of a connection. A few words of comfort from a loved one, a telling fact that convinces you that it's them talking to you from the other side." Around the table a number of heads nodded. "Well, it's a lie," he said. "A charade founded on mumbo-jumbo and wishful thinking."

The exclamations of puffed-up, put-on distress made me smile.

"What we think of as spirits," Gilfillan went on with an erudition belied by his appearance (I was beginning to think of him as perhaps a university professor fallen on hard times) "are simply echoes of personalities trapped in dislocated pockets of time. Usually the result of a sudden, unexpected death – unexpected most of all by the victim – these partials are semi-aware, but no more than a sliver of the person they once were." Margaret and her ladies were nodding sagely, even though the Australian's bunk practically equated to 'there are no such things as ghosts'. To my right, Helen disguised a snigger behind a sneeze.

"To effect a genuine communication with these spirit remnants," Gilfillan droned on, "requires them to be local in both the temporal and the spatial dimensions." His head swivelled as he regarded his audience. "Have any of you suffered a recent loss, I wonder?"

"I lost a good cashmere mitten last week," Helen said sweetly.

Margaret fired us a look, and I squeezed Helen's hand, both in gentle admonishment and in admiration.

"Well, I really would love to find it again," she murmured in my ear. "I mean, what use is a single mitten to anybody?"

Around the table a number of lace-gloved hands had gone up.

Gilfillan ignored the interruption. "Of course, by *recent*, I should specify, within the last week or so."

The hands went down again.

"Very well," Gilfillan said. "We shall just have to see what

happens. But I will not guarantee the specificity of the results."
He leaned across the table and whipped away the cloth.

The apparatus was assembled mostly of a framework of drilled struts fixed together with odd bolts, wing-nuts and washers. Within this framework was cradled a bakelite box with no features apart from the cluster of terminals that connected it to a good sized electrical motor via a ripped knitting of kinked and twisted wires. The remaining space was taken up by a large battery cell.

"What you are about to witness," the Australian declared, "is no *Ouija*, no *ectoplasm*, no *moving table* or any other such tricks. Stripped of mysticism, divorced from religion, this is nothing less than science. The science of temporal co-planar collocation."

You had to give him his due. He made this baffling drivel sound impressive.

From the speed that he went about making his apparatus actually do something, however, I surmised that this must have been the bit of his spiel that patrons usually started asking for their money back. With a shower of fat, acrid-smelling sparks he connected the motor to the battery and it emitted a whirring sound, quickly winding itself up into a whine that vibrated the table and rattled the drops of the chandeliers.

Then I felt a tugging sensation, a lurch similar to that felt on a train that is leaving a station. One of the ladies gave a small cry.

"No worries," Gilfillan half-shouted above the din. "We're just getting up to speed so that the apparatus can locate the nearest available spook."

I felt the lurch again and it seemed to me that I must have been straining my eyesight in the dim light for too long because I began to see gold sparkles, similar to the bright dust motes that get illuminated by a shaft of sunlight. Only, there was no such light in the dining room's brown gloom.
Before long the room was filled with cascading showers of the golden sparks.

"Ooh, pretty." I heard Helen murmur, but her voice seemed disorientatingly distant.

The whine of the motor rose in pitch and I felt that lurch again, stronger than before, a yank to the guts that made me feel dizzy and quite nauseated.

And then the apparatus ceased. Someone gasped in the vacuum, a sort of wordless sigh of surprise.

"Ah," Gilfillan said. "Here we are now."

I suppose, that was the moment that I could have done something. Disconnected the machine, whatever, just made it stop. I was certainly no longer enjoying the experience, and I wish I'd had the presence of mind to take Helen by the hand and leave. If I choose to believe Gilfillan's explanation of the theory of his machine, it would have made no difference to what was to follow, but I can never escape the feeling that I allowed it to happen.

The sparks faded from the air, and in their place a bright figure coalesced above the table: a shining blur, accompanied by a sound that to me, even without the knowledge of hindsight, was like the hiss of heavy rain. The apparition dazzled too much to be able to make out more than that its shape was female, and that it was as frightened as all hell.

"Who are you, spirit?" Gilfillan asked it.

I saw Margaret lean forward in her chair, face lit with wonder, although she must have known that this was not John.

Its voice was a whisper, and even though the rain sound masked it, I recognised it instantly. It was the voice that whispered love in my ear in the flickering darkness of the Salon cinema. The voice that had lit up with delight, and said, 'yes, yes, I will.'

"Nelly," it said.

My Helen? Only *I* called her 'Nelly'.

Close by, I heard a muffled sigh, a bump, a thump, and only then realised that Helen had fallen to the floor.

I carried her out of the dining room. I knew it was probably unwise to move her, but I wanted her away from that apparatus, and the inexplicable thing it had conjured. Lying her on the settee in the parlour, I feared the worst when I saw how pale, how still, she was... and I hugged her with relief when she finally responded to my fevered pinching with a spirited, "all, right! I've not passed over yet!"

To Margaret's credit, she cleared the house of guests and spiritualist alike and made Helen comfortable until she recovered sufficiently from her faint for me to take her home. The apparition was mentioned only by Helen, who later miraculously rationalised the whole affair.

"Well he was getting his own back on me, of course," she told me a day or so later as we wandered through a frosty Kelvingrove. "Putting the wind up the unbeliever. Very effective too. That'll teach me to cross swords with a spiritualist. Decent piece of mimicry too, don't you think? Sounded just like me."

It had sounded far too like her. For a horrible minute that piece of mischievous ventriloquism had convinced me of the impossible. But I could feel the heat of her hands through her new cashmere mittens. My Helen was no ghost, and we went home that day to begin planning our wedding.

Then she was killed.

Went out for messages in a rainstorm. Slipped on loose cobbles on the Broomielaw and drowned in the Clyde.

Simple as that. It was ten days since she and I had seen her ghost hovering above Gilfillan's *Time Machine*. What else would you call that apparatus? A device that searches for the nearest sundered spirit. Nearest in time. Backwards or forwards. *Past or future*.

I have said that I don't believe in ghosts, but over the years there have been times... There *are* times still when I visit the house on Partick Hill, and Margaret lays the board out on that same table, and we dim the lights and place our two paper-thin hands on the planchette. And we take turns asking our questions of the night, but no-one is there to answer.

The Bennie and The Bonobo

George Bennie watched the future glide to a halt on the track above his head. He smiled. Waiting at the foot of the gantry stairs as the invited dignitaries and potential investors disembarked from his gleaming railplane, he grinned. And he beamed at the excited chatter that he could hear over the purr of the fore and aft prop screws easing down to a lazy birl.

He was going to be vindicated. Applauded. Rich.

It was 1930 and, with the wounds of the Great War beginning to heal at last, the country was ready to move on. And what better way to do that than replace the ponderous, dirty railways with this sleek, elevated wonder? People had a right to travel in speed and comfort.

The queue of passengers reached him. Hands pumped his, faces glowed, lips spilled excitable platitudes.

Such a smooth ride.

Bennie felt the charge off them, the genuine thrill.

159

Neil Williamson

The stained glass windows are darling.

And every single one of these people had influence, would carry away the message that the Bennie Railplane was the mode of tomorrow, and anyone not on board with a sizeable investment would be left behind in the past.

Imagine, Glasgow to Edinburgh in twenty minutes.

And all this from a public demonstration in a sidings in Milngavie. There was so much more he could do to refine the design. The engines for instance, now just a pair of standard, noisy diesels...

"It'll never happen."

The voice – soft, female, American – snapped him out of his thoughts. The rest of the passengers, having made their congratulations were now trudging back towards the offices, leaving a lone figure: really no taller than a child, shawled and bonneted so that her face could not be seen, and hands in a muff, which Bennie thought odd for July. Mentally he scanned the passenger list – of course, it was the widow from New York, the late addition: Mrs... Mrs... *Blanchflower*, that was it.

It seemed she alone had not been impressed by the railplane's demonstration. Well, that was hardly surprising for an American. They were never impressed by anything they hadn't made themselves.

Bennie adopted his most reassuring tone. "I guarantee you, Madam, the concept is sound, and the vehicle perfectly safe."

"Oh, I know it is," replied the voice from the bonnet. "But even still your dream will be strangled. You will die a broken and destitute man."

With that outburst, the tiny woman hirpled away, as if plagued by bad joints, in the direction of an open workshop door. Bridling, but beginning to suspect this antagonism as that of a competitor's investor come to inspect the opposition and finding it frustratingly superior, Bennie followed. It took a moment to spot her in the dimness, but there she was, in the

160

lee of a stripped-down engine block.

"I should warn you," he began, "that my designs are fully patented – "

She removed a hand from her muff, holding it up to stop him. He stared at the hand. It was long-fingered and covered in thick black hair.

The hand loosened the ties of the bonnet, slipped it back. If she had not silenced him, the face which was revealed would have left him speechless anyway. Huge chocolate eyes under bony brows, a toothy mouth, wide nostrils, and more of that strange hair.

In his astonishment Bennie couldn't help himself. "You're a mon– "

The visitor bared impressive teeth with a soft growl.

Bennie realized his taxonomical mistake. "Sorry, a chim– "

"If I had been a *'chim'*, I'd have bitten your testicles off at *'mon'*." She sighed. "The word you are looking for, George, is *bonobo*. Other side of the Congo River from the *chims*. Look, we don't have time for lengthy explanations, but I can see you will need an explanation of *me* before we can progress to the matter at hand." The ape stroked the hair under her chin, as if choosing her next words with care. "In the future," she said, "humans will find ways to make modifications to the body that would make your hair stand on end. Literally, if that's what you desire."

Bennie's hand went reflexively to smooth his receding Brylcreemed hair.

"Where I come from, they can – and you'd better believe they do – boost and alter any physical human attribute you can name."

The obvious question dutifully formed on his lips. "Then you're not *really* a mon...?"

She was ready for it. "A *bonobo*," she repeated. "Yes, I am. *Of course*, they had to experiment on someone else before they were allowed to go to town on human bodies, didn't they? I may be fourth-generation enhanced, but I'm still one hundred per cent bonobo, thank you."

Bennie, not yet close to appreciating any of the bewildering volley of concepts that had been hurled at him in the last few minutes, did manage to catch the inference in this. Four generations of radical genetic experimentation must have produced a lot of dead-ends before they got it right. "I'm sorry," he said.

"Don't be," she said matter-of-factly. "I'm more intelligent than the average human. And I've got my own apartment in the East Village, not to mention a research grant. I've even got the vote, although given that it's still only white human males that ever make it to the election platform it's frankly no use to me at all. They'd be better off with chimps."

"Did you say, the *future*?"

The bonobo scratched her nose. "Catch on fast, don't you? How else would I know that your beautiful railplane is doomed to failure?"

"Please don't keep saying that." Bennie felt unwell. His head was light and his stomach was hollow, and he felt as if, just as he had been gathering momentum down the gleaming railway track of his life, someone had switched the points and diverted him into a most peculiar siding. In such circumstances there was only one thing for an engineer to do: throw the vehicle into reverse, and back up carefully to rejoin the main line.

"Well, Mrs Blanchflower," he said. Ignoring the disturbing question of who *Mr Blanchflower* might be, he smiled more brightly than he felt able and took one step, two, back towards the door. "Many thanks for coming to my little demonstration. I'm sorry you've come so far only to be disappointed. However, you will understand that I have a number of other guests, who I seem to be neglecting – "

"Nineteen fifty-seven."

"I'm sorry?" The ape had the rather irritating habit of blowing up the tracks in front of his train of thought.

"I didn't mean to put it so bluntly," she said softly, "but that's the year you will die. Having spent all of your money on travelling the world looking for investors in the railplane, you eventually give up and take over the running of a small shop to make ends meet. The year before you die, this demonstration track, along with the carriage that sits on it right now, which will have been rusting flake by brittle flake among the gorse bushes and weeds for more than twenty-five years, will finally be dismantled. That's when the dream that has been worn down to a hard nugget inside your heart will finally wear so thin that it'll break and vanish. You won't live another year after that."

Part of Bennie's brain had been aware all along that he really shouldn't be standing talking to an ape in a dress, especially one with such an eloquent – even lyrical – turn of phrase, but that part was overruled by the part that took umbrage at the decidedly insulting tone to her speech. "I'm sorry, madam," he said stiffly. "The evidence is to the contrary. I have a number of *very firm* expressions of interest already, and..." His composure broke. "*By Christ*, did you see the looks on their faces? Did you hear what they were saying? They're up at my office right now, stuffing themselves with French canapés and waiting to throw money at me."

The bonobo simply shook her head, a sort of mournful look in her soft, brown eyes.

"Well, give me a reason then," Bennie blustered. "What's to stop them?"

"There's a war coming."

"Ha!" Now he knew what this was: A prank! His visitor was nothing more than an actress in an ape costume – a very convincing one, granted – her acting, however, was far more persuasive than her grasp of world affairs. "A war indeed. Who put you up to this? It's barely a decade since we won the war to end all wars. There will be naught but peace and prosperity for the rest of our lifetimes."

"So you say," she replied, unfazed, "but nevertheless, there

163

is one coming, and before the decade is out. And what's more it'll be worse than the last one."

"Nonsense." In the face of her calm conviction, this didn't even sound convincing to his own ears.

"And it's not just the war. The railway owners will call in favours with persons of influence. With all this apparent peace and prosperity you're talking about, business is looking good for them. The last thing they need is a cheaper, faster, altogether better alternative to the train."

"When the railplane network is in place there will still be a role for the traditional railways," Bennie protested, but he'd used that argument so often that, true as it was – the railplane would only ever be suitable for express passenger conveyance – it sounded glib even to him.

"George," the bonobo blinked, and wiped at her eye in such a natural and non-human fashion that Bennie's brief fantasy about the actress in the ape suit was blown apart like a dandelion head in the wind. "Do you really think they'll be content with *goods haulage?*"

The logical part of Bennie's brain gained the upper hand then: and it found her argument, if not persuasive, then at least coherent. Even likely.

Bennie pulled up a three-legged stool and sat on it, clasping his hands in front of his eyes. Was it really possible that all his bright plans would come to nothing? He felt warm fingers, soft as leather gloves pat his head. A gentle squeeze of solidarity.

"Very well," he said at length. "Assuming that I take you at your word – that you are an intelligent ape that has come from the future to ruin my entire life just at its happiest moment to date. But I have to ask you: Why? What have I done that you should hate me so much?"

"That's complicated, George."

A muffling of her voice made him open his eyes and look. She was nowhere to be seen.

"I certainly hated you at one point," she continued. The voice was coming from behind a row of lathes and pedestal drills. "Or at least hated you in *principle*. In much the same way as pretty soon you'll grow to hate the railway owners." There was a grunt of effort and the sound of something heavy being dragged on the floor. "But now I know how things are, I empathize." As Bennie approached the bank of machines, the ape's head suddenly popped up.

She smiled in a not particularly wholesome fashion. "We're the same, you see? So, I've not come to ruin your life, but to offer you ... something which should help." Mrs Blanchflower ducked down again, and apparently did something that began a noise like rice grains being dropped onto a skillet.

Bennie didn't see. How he could be considered in any way the same as this perplexing creature, he had no idea. Then, as he got a clear sight of what was behind the lathes, a glimmer of understanding was finally lit.

Mrs Blanchflower had dragged a rusting bogey assembly into an empty area of the floor. She looked up from a device cradled in her hairy hand. "You don't need this, do you?" She indicated the scrap.

Bennie shook his head.

"Good, iron is about as good as we could hope for here for a substrate."

Something was happening to the old bogey. The metal was flowing, beading like condensation and dripping to the floor in a rattling rain of spherules that bounced and rolled in all directions. Mrs Blanchflower tapped at her device and the skittering balls underwent a miraculous change in direction, reversing and converging on a structure that, as he watched, was rapidly rising from the floor.

Bennie watched with admiration as balls flowed together into strands that entwined, becoming cables that rose up like charmed snakes and met at the top to form a shape recognizable as a doorway.

"What's this then?" he asked.

165

"This?" the ape said, stepping over what was left of the pile of scrap to inspect the completed arch. "This will take you to any point on the planet, and as I discovered by accident during the development phase, any point in history."

Bennie peered at the iron archway. This was what she had meant when she said they were the same. The ape was an engineer. "You designed this ... process?"

She bobbed her head. "Indeed. You just tell it where you want to be, and there you are. It's the transport of the future." She paused, looked at him in a curious fashion with her unreadable, inhuman eyes. "Or at least *a* future."

"What do you mean by that?"

"It's best if I show you."

"It's *best* if you tell me," Bennie replied. As far as he could see, the archway was only that. Standing a little off true, and with something of a kink near the apex, it resembled modern sculpture more than any mode of transport he had seen. Yet, close to it, there was a charge in the air, a potential, that made him cautious.

Mrs Blanchflower sighed, looked at the floor. "I have a confession to make," she said.

"Yes?"

"The reason I came here was to stop you. Stop the railplane before it ever got developed. Originally, I mean."

Bennie shook his head. "I thought you said the whole project was doomed to failure?" he said, bitterly.

"For the most part, yes it is." She shuffled, less confident now than she had been earlier. "George, I didn't know until I came back, but my future is one of the very, very few where you did succeed."

"Your future? You mean there's more than one?"

She shrugged, an odd gesture he thought for an ape. "Potentially infinite futures. But it turns out most events coalesce towards one probable outcome. I've been to 1957 – dozens of times, by dozens of routes – and the outcome's always the same.

You should have been designing a new kind of engine then that was going to give the bennie a real edge over the train, but all I found was a rusting heap on the sidings and a disillusioned inventor."

Bennie stuck his hands in his pockets, walked away from the bonobo. This was madness. Twenty minutes ago he had been watching the evidence of his assured fame with his own eyes. It was a *certainty*. It was in the sunbeams bouncing off the polished steel carriage and it was in the faces of the passengers. How could it not be, after all this time, all this hard work? And yet, he had already had prickly dealings with the railways. *He felt his certainty crack.* And if the world did indeed go to war again so soon... *He felt it crumble.* There'd be no investment, not even from the Americans. *He swore he* heard *it crash.*

Mrs Blanchflower must have heard it too. "You see," she said softly, "we're the same."

Bennie rounded on her then, finding that anger had replaced the denial. "Exactly *how*, madam, can we be considered *the same*..." he began.

It was that sad look in her eyes again that killed the anger as quickly as it had arisen. "Because in *my* future, George, the one that's virtually impossible to locate unless you already came from there and know how to get back – the one where, despite everything, you did succeed – it's the centuries-long, world-wide dominance of the Bennie Transport Corporation that stifles new ideas, new inventions – like this one, yes – if there's even a possibility that they might challenge a fraction of its monopoly."

Mrs Blanchflower stepped in front of the archway and held out her hand. "Would you like to see?"

*

The future was exactly as Bennie had dreamed it. Glasgow had grown larger, taller, brighter, and its four great railway stations had become the looms for gigantic silver ribbons of clustered bennie lines that spun out of the city to the north, the east, the south and the west; to the rest of Scotland, and the United Kingdom, and via miraculous bridges to Europe, and beyond.

Their journey across the Atlantic would take no more than an hour and a half. Bennie had wanted to stay in Glasgow, but Mrs Blanchflower pointed out, somewhat peevishly but correctly enough, that there was nothing left there of the city he knew in his time.

Since they had arrived in the future, the bonobo had become withdrawn. She clearly had plans she wanted to be getting on with. It was as well, then, to accompany her to New York. If he wanted to come back later it was only a short hop after all.

The view from the upper level of the triple-decker behemoth as it zephyred along the gentle sine of its track was stunning. The great grey North Atlantic reared and swirled as a storm raged below them. Rain rattled against the observation windows, but the megabennie – as he was told it was called, and he was pleased to recognize many similarities to his original design despite the various improvements that had been made – continued on, smooth and true.

Marvellous.

Mrs Blanchflower coughed to attract his attention. That was when he realized that the rattling he had heard was not the rain. She had pulled up a section of deep-pile carpet and was busy turning a square of metal decking into another of her archways.

"I thought I was going to see New York," Bennie said, disappointed that she was sending him home already. Home, it was suggested, to humiliation and failure. She'd shown him 1957. It had been horrible.

"This isn't for you," she said, and nodded to the chair next to his. Where she had been sitting, there was a plastic card. "The keys to my apartment and my bank account," she said. "It's not much, I'm afraid, but then you know how it is being a struggling genius and all."

So he was staying here? But that meant...

168

"What are you going to do?" Bennie asked.

That sad look came over her face again. "This is *your* future, George," she said. "I'm off in search of *mine*."

She was wrong on that account, or at least unspecific. This wasn't *his* future, or that of thousands of other versions of himself, but it was the future of some randomly favoured George Bennie who had somehow fluked his dream into actuality. Since this remarkable trip had begun, he had clung to the slenderest hope that he would return to his 1930 and, armed with the certainty that his vision could be fulfilled, would make it so. The very fact that Mrs Blanchflower was leaving him here with no opportunity of return, and that *here*, and in particular the vehicle he rode on, still existed, proved that it wasn't he after all who had succeeded.

Bennie appreciated the fact that she didn't make any more fuss than that. One minute the talking ape was standing beside her invention, the next ... the archway encompassed her in a complex and quite frightening folding motion and both she and it were gone.

Bennie stared at the hole in the floor, and the two stumps of slag that marked where it had stood. *Where's the elegance in that?* he thought. *It'll never catch on.*

Then he settled back in his seat and enjoyed the rest of his trip to the capital of a New World where they clearly knew a good prospect when they saw it.

A Horse In Drifting Light

I wanted a change of scene. Something more than these four walls. Don't get me wrong, the apartment is fantastic – the company is good in that respect – but it was slowly driving me crazy. Little things – the mark on the living room wall that showed through any decoration, the too-cheerful chime of incoming work, the fridge's thing about ordering olives. It used to order a jar of olives every week. Green, black, stuffed with pimentos. Obviously the previous tenant was something of a fan. Me, I can't stand them. They leave a bad taste. I'd reprogrammed the fridge countless times. Mostly my groceries are olive-free now but the occasional jar still manages to sneak its way in. Like I say, little things but when you spend your entire day on your own in the one place it gets to you. It was definitely getting to me.

I could have taken the underground down to Knightswood where the company kept an office for those who expressed a preference for enjoying the 'social aspects of their work', but usually they turned out to be refugees from bad home situations who made sure they brought their problems to work with them. Keeping clear of that type was the number one reason most people elected for the home office package.

Possibly it was getting close to time to request a transfer again. Novalogue had manufactories on five continents and I'd been based at the Glasgow hub for six years now, but I knew they wouldn't sanction it until I'd sorted out the production problems in Sao Paolo.

Same went double for a holiday.

Knowing all this made each day in the flat increasingly difficult to bear. An interim solution had to be found.

The idea lodged itself in my brain following a drunken evening with Des from Seattle. Wednesday night, football night. We'd drunk a few beers and after the match – one of us bitching, the other crowing in our usual friendly kind of way – the conversation had turned to cars, the old kind people drove around by themselves.

"They were beautiful," Des slurred, his image freezing and skipping momentarily, indicating a surge in server loading. Probably the Japanese evening recreation traffic kicking in. I popped up a clock. Sure enough it was that late. As if triggered by the knowledge, I felt a wave of fatigue.

"Des," I yawned. "Everyone knows they were wasteful, environmentally unsound and dangerous as hell. That's why they were banned in every civilised country."

Des grunted.

"Besides," I went on. "Society doesn't need them now. Everything you want can be delivered to your door. Anyone you want to speak to, anywhere in the world, you can do from your favourite chair. Any place you want to go there's transport that can take you. I remember cars, even if unlike you I wasn't old enough to drive before they were gone. Des, I don't miss them. I don't miss the fumes or the gridlock or the daily RTA reports. Come on, mate, move with the times. They're gone. Forget them."

He peered at me. "Gordon," he sighed, and I thought there was some deep misery exposed then on his face. "You don't understand, son. When you were driving you had freedom, you felt in control of your life. You know what I mean? Not just where you were going, but every second of the journey. At every junction, around every corner, over every bump and hole in the road. You had control. Today, we're all just passengers and the world overtakes us. Leaves us behind."

I didn't know how to respond to that. A bubble of silence stretched thin before Des popped it with some noncommittal dissembling, a joke or something, I don't remember. We logged off shortly after and I went to bed with a new hollowness in me, but also the germ of an idea.

So this was how I came to be in a car motoring through the countryside south of the city. Obviously it wasn't the kind of car that Des was nostalgic for. This could more accurately be called a private transport bus. Exorbitantly expensive, but for the sake of my mental health I figured it was worth it. I requested a route that would take me out of the city for the day and back again, but otherwise was random. I didn't care where I went as long as the scenery kept changing. At one point I passed wide fields packed with a plant in bloom, its blossom a heavily saturated yellow with a substantial content of green. The effect was bright but somewhat sickly.

Rape, the car told me. GM'd to manufacture insulin.

At least it was different. I quickly found myself able to relax and enjoy the journey.

Most of my meetings that day passed without anyone remarking on my change of surroundings, although Angelina at the Brazilian Head Office did ask about the electric hum in the background. When I told her the reason, she looked puzzled and said, "Oh."

Around mid-day I got the car to stop two-thirds or so of the way up a hill. I climbed out to stretch my legs and eat a sandwich from the selection in the fridge.

Neil Williamson

The sky was enormous. It seemed silly but seeing it unbounded by the regular framework of the city's buildings I couldn't believe there was so much of it. The sun blazed down from the summit of the hill, warming my neck as I watched clouds shift across the valley below me. I was surprised to be made aware, it felt possibly for the first time in my life, of the three dimensional nature of the sky; low cumulus scudding quickly, towering cirrus passing more slowly. The clouds passed over fields, a wide river, and, further away, a town of some size. My memory suggested that it might be Hamilton, but having never seen it from the outside, I wasn't sure. The air was big too. I breathed in a deep lungful, sampling the freshness laced with a number of sweet flavours for which I had no name.

For the first time that I could remember I smiled in my own company.

I walked a little further up the hill. The road was uneven, pitted. A ditch ran roadside of a leafy hedge. I stopped when I came to a break in it. An iron gate barred the way into a steep field of pasture. At first I thought the field empty but then my attention was snagged by something, a bright movement. Standing perfectly still some distance up the slope, I guessed a couple of hundred metres, was an animal, a horse. As if sensing my presence, it tossed its head and began to trot down towards the gate.

At first I though the beast was on fire.

The sun sparkled and danced off its hide, spears of light lancing in arbitrary directions like an old disco glitterball. I watched the animal's leisurely progress in awe. It trotted at a genteel pace, stopping often to look around or investigate the grass. Certainly it didn't seem to be in pain.

The horse stopped in front of me, bobbed its head a couple of times over the gate, fixed me with a large blue eye. Blinked. I could not understand what I was seeing. In all respects the animal had the characteristics of a horse except that its coat was silvered. No, mirrored. Like chrome. I couldn't discern any individual hairs. I was suspicious of the eye colour too.

174

A Horse In Drifting Light

What did I know of horses? I'd never seen one in real life but I'd seen them in movies. Westerns and such. The closest experience I had was when I was very young. My mother took me once to the beach at Largs. There were donkey rides. An anachronistic form of entertainment even then. Possibly for the sake of novelty I was forced onto the back of an animal which was then dragged by its owner up the beach, turned around and back to my waiting mother. I remember feeling with my knees the outline of bones beneath warm, yeasty smelling skin, coarse hair rubbing against my bare legs, the black thatch of mane I clutched for dear life, the glistening of drool on the shiny metal bit in its mouth, the flies that buzzed around its docile big head. I remember the relief as I was lifted off, which voiced itself in the tantrum I kicked up as I was returned to my mother.

This creature smelled of nothing. Its mane and slowly swishing tail looked like very expensive Christmas tinsel. It snickered as I put out my hand, exposing a far more plausible mouth, all tongue and yellow teeth, but allowed me to touch it. Its skin was warm, but less like skin than extremely pliable aluminium. Its breath was warm on my face.

The horse demonstrated itself tame by allowing me to continue clapping it. I imagined perhaps it even enjoyed the attention but I really couldn't tell. I watched the sky mirrored in its flanks, the sun dazzling from chinks in the clouds which passed across its hide like time. We stayed like that, spellbound, until a large drop of rain, pregnant with encapsulated sky, broke on its brow, rolled smoothly down its long face. That drop was chased by another, and another. Became a flurry, then a downpour.

The horse stamped once, tossed its sparkling mane and turned away. A poem of fluid natural movement, it raced up the hill, its powerful legs carrying it out of sight in no time.

Realising I was soaked I went back to the car, and the car dried me and provided a warm drink, and sped me home by the shortest possible route.

And I let it.

Sins of the Father
[co-written with Mark Roberts]

Sandor's final clue was a bottle of rain. I had trailed him across half the world, from Bucharest to Palo Alto, from Brisbane to Jakarta, to this village on the edge of the jungle. I had tried to guess his intent, like a haruspex, from the flotsam littering his wake – the credit trail, hotel bookings and phone calls; the hired 4x4 dumped at a private airfield in Monterrey, the bewildered girlfriend, abandoned in Basle. While his purpose remained a mystery, I had become increasingly certain of his destination, and knew it was imperative that I stop him reaching it.

Now, this bare hut: a low bed in the corner, a bowl and jug for washing. But no trace of my son. I gulped humid air to suppress a surge of panic, and forcibly reminded myself that I had built a career, a life, on my facility for clear thinking and decisive action. A beat passed, soft jungle sounds outside. The panic passed too. There is always one more thing to try.

Under the bedding I found maps, printouts and a metal case sporting a faded sticker. Global Weather Watch – the charity for whom Sandor had most recently been chasing weather systems. The case contained two rows of slender bottles pressed into a block of stiff foam. Each had a scrawled label. I held one up to the light for better examination. The liquid inside was clear, with a tint of amber, and I could see suspended in it particles of some dark material. I unstoppered the bottle, inhaled – and recoiled. The vapour flooded my nasal passages, a cold rush burning through my sinuses like menthol, leaving a delicate chemical sweetness. The shock of the odour appeared to induce some kind of synaesthetic episode. For a dizzying instant the smell transformed into a sound like the distant falling of heavy rain, and the walls of the hut seemed to recede unsteadily. I screwed my eyes shut, and sat on the bed until my head cleared sufficiently to trust my vision again.

Examining the label, I managed to discern a word, followed by a date and a set of co-ordinates.

Precipitation? This aromatic liquid was rain? From where, Chernobyl?

Equally troubling was that I could not identify this as Sandor's handwriting. Did the P in *Precipitation* match those in *Happy Birthday, Papa*? He had stopped sending me birthday cards long ago. I dismissed that train of thought and re-focussed on the problem at hand. It was all the more urgent now. If Sandor had left these things behind it meant he had found what he was looking for.

I returned to the printouts and the maps. The co-ordinates marked in black biro tied up with those written on some of the bottles.

Footsteps behind me. "Where now?" asked Joshua.

I thrust a map into his hands, poked my finger at an X scored so melodramatically that the paper had ripped. "Take me here."

The ex-Ghurkha looked, jaw working his gum.

"That's difficult. It's a gorge, a hell-deep one. Reckon our best bet is to raft down over the falls." His black eyes met mine, held them steadily. "It's difficult," he repeated.

"Make it happen." When he did not depart I said, "There is something you wish to add?"

Softly, he said, "Fifty-fifty they didn't survive the descent." As if I hadn't comprehended what he was saying about the danger. I thought he knew me better than that.

I looked off into the jungle, regarding the wall of colour and shadow as I picked my shirt away from damp skin. "My son," I said, "has been participating in dangerous sports of one sort or another since he was twelve. Abseiling, caving, rafting, base-jumping – it seems he excels at them all. I don't expect him to fail. What concerns me is that he will succeed."

I did not elaborate, although Joshua deserved more. I felt his scrutiny for a moment longer before he left. Perhaps I should have told him the truth, given him the chance to walk away, but I was concerned only for Sandor, and in this forsaken place I needed Joshua's help. Besides, as it turned out, at that moment I had no better idea of the truth than he did.

I had fallen into a reverie. I came out of it when I noticed that the particular patch of shadowy foliage I had been staring at now contained a pair of bright eyes. They blinked lazily, and in one fluid motion a hairy, simian shape swung into view. I have never been fond of animals generally, but I particularly dislike apes and monkeys. No animal should be so close to human, and yet so alien. As I watched, the creature bared its teeth in an impudent grin. Then in a flurry of leaves it was gone.

There was nothing in it, of course, but the encounter seeded me with an unease that would linger for the rest of that evening. Later, sleepless in the livid darkness, I shivered despite the damp heat and, as I have done nightly all of my adult life, faced my fears.

I feared for my son. I had been, at best, a distant father. Sandor had grown up headstrong, constantly waging small rebellions, working his way through a string of paid tutors, but

Neil Williamson

he had always been good-hearted. That he had, for some reason, now progressed to theft was not the problem. I feared because of the thing stolen. The stone torus I had liberated from the Durrant collection in Massachusetts. As I drifted off to sleep, I recalled acutely the comfortable weight of the torus in my hand: the seductive smoothness, greasy like soap but firm as granite. And I feared that Sandor had experienced that same repulsive attraction. It was a fear lacking any concrete rationale – this was only a piece of stone, after all – but inexplicable as it was, the fear was real, and it had grown in me the longer this search had gone on.

*

The journey to the gorge the following morning proved as unpleasant as I had feared. The heat and humidity may well have been tolerable, but the density of the foliage, the persistent attacks of insects, the unevenness of the ground made the going difficult. We travelled in resentful silence.

I expected things to get easier once we were on the river, but it was worse. For the greater part, we found ourselves exposed to an unrelenting sun, and I felt the skin at my temples and back of my neck grow tight and red. As our sturdy inflatable drifted out into the flow I wondered if Joshua had taken us to the correct river, but I should have known better than to doubt him. It wasn't long before the current began to tug more insistently. Soon I could make out the roar of white water up ahead.

"Are you ready, Mr. Weinhardt?" Joshua asked, half turning. Before I could reply, we hit the rapids. The boat pitched wildly, soaking us with spume. Over the next few minutes keeping ourselves afloat demanded such concentration that we were half over the edge of the falls before I was aware of it. There was an absurd weightless moment when the world was all spray and silent sky, during which I found time to be glad our kit was secured and watertight. Then we were falling towards a frothing pool, eighty feet below.

180

I had rehearsed the moment in my mind and had firmly decided to hold fast to the boat as we descended, but Joshua flung himself free of the vessel with a wild cry as it dropped over the lip of the falls. I experienced an instant of terrific indecision. Then, already feeling like I was flying, I kicked away from the dinghy and tumbled forwards.

I struck the water shoulder first with a thunderous slap. For what felt like minutes there was only the dark silence of the water and my heart beating hard in my aching chest. Part of me wondered what it would be like to drown, and considered that perhaps it would not be so bad to die like that, in a tranquil pool in Borneo. I was not afraid of death. I had faced that fear long ago, and the world had shown me much of it since. When I thought about death at all, I had begun secretly to find the idea of such release attractive. Something I had earned. But there would be no such peace for me now – not if it meant leaving my son in danger. With a tiny measure of reluctance I kicked against the water and rose towards the light, surfacing back in the roaring world of the waterfall.

Joshua had already reached the dinghy and was dragging it to the shore. I swam over and helped him, then the two of us hauled ourselves onto the rocky bank. When I suggested we rest there to dry out a little he nodded agreement, fishing some soggy gum out of a shirt pocket.

"Where to now?" I asked after we had secured the dinghy.

Joshua shrugged. "We are *here*," he said, "according to the map."

My gaze shifted to the dense forest, suddenly expecting to see eyes staring back. Many eyes. Of course, there were none.

"Come on," I muttered, annoyed with myself, and pushed off into the jungle.

*

Neil Williamson

The first hour after the falls was dispiriting. As we struggled along, keeping the churning of the river to our left, I became suffused with a sense of futility. Narrow as it was, the gorge was long and we could only search on one side of the river at a time. On top of that, our progress through the vegetation was slow.

Then we found Sandor's boat tucked into a quiet inlet. It was rigid, larger than our own and had been hitched to two trees with blue nylon ropes. A quick inspection revealed that the oars had been carefully stowed and a count of the helmets and jackets indicated that there were six in his party. At least he had come prepared.

My mood soared with an influx of hope. I felt that Sandor was just ahead, that we only had to follow his trail through the jungle to catch up with him. Except there was no trail. Only jungle. There was nothing for it but to continue as we had been.

When the light began to fail we forced our way inland in an effort to avoid the proliferate biting insects that clouded the air along the bank, and made camp. Darkness closed rapidly. By the time we had finished eating, our world had shrunk to a flickering blue circle of electric light. When, inevitably, the lamp began to attract a variety of winged things, large and small, we opted to retire to the tent and net ourselves securely in.

"Mr Weinhart – Andras – what's this all about?"

I lay back, staring upwards so that I would not have to meet Joshua's gaze – all too powerful in the enforced intimacy of the tent. The question surprised me, although it should not have. I had known Joshua since our army days and had had need of his specialist talents to aid my civilian enterprises on a number of occasions since. He was loyal, trustworthy and possessed of a certain cold efficiency, and although the military in him stifled the urge to voice the question, he asked it anyway. Perhaps he was as close to a friend as I had.

Eventually I said, "Sandor stole something. From me. From the collection. Ironic, don't you think?"

Ironic, because this was more than a simple act of childish

182

rebellion. It was his ethical commentary on my profession. Plainly speaking, I have been called a thief – although, I prefer the term *facilitator*. People want things, they come to me and I arrange for those items to be provided. Whatever term was used, it did not sit well with my son. Ever since Sandor learned about what I do, he had assumed an obliquely antagonistic stance according to his own ethical code. The *stealing* – he made it sound so petty – he didn't mind if it was money or jewellery from the enfranchised few, but he became outraged if he discovered my contracts involved public museums and galleries. Robbing the people, he would say. Maybe this had something to do with devoting his energies to charities and his environmental studies, to joining archaeological expeditions, or digging wells for the poor residents of screwed-up little countries like the one to which I had now followed him.

My private collection was an eclectic assortment of pieces that had taken my eye over the years. Much of it was priceless, all of it hard won, and a fair proportion was dedicated to the practice of obscure and sometimes extreme religions. I had long been enthralled by man's inventiveness when it came to having a greater power to believe in, the lengths he would go to in the name of faith. The torus was something else altogether. If angels and devils bookend the visible spectrum of world religions, the piece that Sandor took from my collection was deep into the ultraviolet. I don't know what had attracted him to it but he could hardly have taken anything more – what? What was it about the thing that made my mouth immediately dry at the thought? You only had to look at it to know that it was dangerous. So *very* dangerous. But maybe that was the attraction after all. Perhaps, deep down I thought at the time – and here I freely add arrogance to my sins – there was something of the father in the son after all. I know now that notion could not have been further from the truth.

To Joshua I said, "It was a religious artefact. A round torus of orange stone. It would fit comfortably in the palm of your hand, or could conceivably have been designed to have a thong passed through it for wearing about the neck. Although the surface was worn almost smooth through repeated handling," I wiped my fingers reflexively on my shirt, "there remained faint evidence of writing. It was an unfamiliar script, mixing characters and pictograms. I quickly noticed that one symbolic grouping, suggesting a tower beneath a circle, seemed to have special significance. I was attempting to decipher this text when Sandor took it."

Joshua took a minute, reasoning what I'd said. "And this stone puts him in danger," he said.

It puts us all in danger, I wanted to say, instinctively knowing this for the truth, but unable to rationalize it aloud. "I believe that the artefact was created on this island. I'd imagine that the makers would not take kindly to an outsider possessing one of their sacred objects."

"So, what's the boy's angle?" Joshua asked. "Why bring it back here?"

I had no answer for him. It might have occurred to Sandor to try and return what he saw as a cultural artefact to its rightful owners – I would have loved such a simple explanation – but he *could not have known* that I possessed it, let alone where the thing had originated. The only alternative I could imagine, I found terrifying. Until Sandor had taken the torus, I had made no connection between handling the unpleasant artefact and subsequently finding myself awake at three in the morning, dialling the number of my clandestine travel agent, suddenly inspired to make some trip or other. Now, I was trying to ignore the notion that whatever Sandor had *thought* was his purpose – the rain, everything – was irrelevant; that every choice, every synchronous connection of his journey had somehow been influenced by the stone itself. But that presumed some kind of *intelligence* – either of the stone or of some other agency.

"Joshua, what do you think of evil?" I said.

I felt the slow burn of his scrutiny, then he said, "People do

184

bad things, Andras. You were a soldier. You've seen what goes on. You need to ask about evil?" He paused before adding, "Srebrenica, for example?"

I remembered: watching through field glasses, cold November sun flaring off the windshield of a VW van crawling out of the town at the head of a column of refugees. Had it been on its own the van might have evaded the ambush fire from the new large calibre machine gun we had just delivered. But I doubt it. Ten minutes later, in an atmosphere of clattering after-echoes, the Serb officer smiled, saying to me in clear English, 'a good demonstration.' And I returned his smile, shook his hand and drove away without giving the affair a second thought. A deal done.

As usual, Joshua had hit the mark. I thought about embarking on a 'morality is subjective' stance but I recognised how absurd that would sound and let the conversation die there. I needed him with me in this and didn't want to stretch his credibility in me any further. I focussed on the even sound of his breathing and tried to push from my mind the crowding darkness of the jungle around us, and found myself wondering again about evil. I considered myself world-wise, but in truth I did not know the first thing about it.

*

We set out again at first light. It had rained during the night and the jungle was fresh and vibrant. Our progress was marked by echoing cries and hoots, sometimes in the distance, sometimes – it seemed – right in front of us, but for hours we saw nothing.

Then we came upon the monkeys. Cresting a rise Joshua stopped, motioned for silence. I crept forward to join him, peering through a fan of foliage. A splashing waterfall pooled in the hollow before us. Gathered around the pool were at least four different species of monkeys. They were grooming each other, drinking from the pool, splashing playfully. Then one ambled forward, cupping a large folded leaf which it laid on the ground. It dipped its fingers inside, then withdrew them coated in some kind of black powder. Baring its gums the animal rubbed its fingers around the inside of its mouth. Taking its lead, the others approached in twos and threes, almost reverently taking a finger of the powder and retiring to put it to their mouths.

"What are they doing?" I said to my companion. It had been intended as a whisper but the sound carried. As one the monkeys looked directly up at us and started jumping up and down with a furious whooping and screaming. Their eyes glared intelligently and their bared teeth blazed white. The instant they rushed the slope, the thundercrack of Joshua's pistol sounded beside me. By the time the reverberations had died away, the hollow had been long emptied. My ears ached.

*

It was another two hours before we discovered the plane. A twin prop passenger crate, its white paint work assuming a slow organic camouflage as it accumulated layers of animal and vegetable secretions. Furthermore, though the plane had evidently crashed here some time ago, it was relatively intact. It was as if the jungle itself had cushioned its fall, and then, in saving the occupants, had condemned them to a slower death as they discovered themselves unable to escape its sinewy boughs, its suffocating humidity.

Nevertheless, I interpreted this latest encounter as good news. Although I did not see how they could be connected, after the boat and the monkeys, this new discovery felt like another marker along our journey. A sign that we were getting closer.

While Joshua explored the cockpit, I circled around – and stopped, amazed. Finger-painted onto the fuselage in some dirty, yellowish substance was a pictogram. I recognised it immediately as a variation of the tower and circle motif. Even incomplete, my studies led me to believe that this pictogram represented an opening

186

within the tower; with a fan of straight lines linking the circle above the tower to the apex. Possibly, I had guessed, representing the rays of the sun or the moon.

There was an open hatch along the side of the plane. Even more curious now, I stuck my head inside. In the dimness I heard rather than saw movement, and something struck me hard across the temple. Soundlessly, I fell backward, blinking in shock. On my back on the jungle floor, I looked up at the canopy, eyesight swimming. A shape moved into view above me, a shape with matted red fur.

Groggily, I realised I had disturbed a juvenile orang-utan who had been exploring the wreck. It leaned over me, peering into my eyes with perfectly evident intelligence. Its own eyes gleamed like polished black marbles, and, making soft noises, it reached out and gently brushed my face with fingers thick with some tacky substance. Then, in my dazed state, I imagined its lips formed a clear word, gently spoken but in an ugly language that I recognised instantly but had never thought I would hear. I wished I hadn't. Reading it was bad enough.

As I looked up at the ape, it smiled at me. Then one side of the animal's face exploded, spraying me with gore. I gasped, scrambling to sit up as the corpse of the ape fell to one side. Joshua stood close by, pistol aimed steadily at the creature in case it was still alive.

"Are you alright?" he asked flatly, although I thought I detected some amusement.

I couldn't answer immediately. I felt warmth on my lips, tasted blood. Seized by a sudden desire to wash my face and neck, I got up too quickly, only to slump again.

Then I saw the heads, and was shocked into lucidity.

"What?" Joshua saw my expression and followed my gaze to the spikes driven into the ground.

He muttered something in his native tongue as he helped me to my feet. I stumbled over to the hideous display. These heads were fresh, too recent to have belonged to the crew of the plane.

My gaze lurched from one decapitated skull to the next, searching pathetically for the head of my son. It was a task which demanded closer scrutiny than I could at that moment bear to give. The heads had been torn from their bodies, the faces agonised masks, like props from a horror film. Eyes were missing, noses and cheeks, torn flaps of skin. I counted, and counted again. Five heads. That left one.

I fell to the ground, helpless as I retched bile, and the last of my self-esteem, into the undergrowth.

Joshua prowled edgily while I collected my wits. At least I now knew for sure that there was more to my unnerved state than simple isolation from civilization and a guilt-fuelled imagination. We were not alone in this jungle. The plane had been completely stripped, all the instruments, seats, everything inside, gone. And the murdered men had not been killed by mere animals – the sickening presentation of their crudely removed heads proved that. My own head throbbed with the thought that we had arrived too late. If indeed these victims had made up Sandor's party, he too, surely, had been slain. Even if he had escaped the initial attack he surely could not have evaded his attackers for long. I was in no doubt that my son had encountered the cultists who had fashioned the torus, and he had been led here as a direct result of my actions. By stealing the torus, I had made this possible. That knowledge sat inside me like a glass bubble. When it broke, there would be shards of pain, the emptiness of grief, but for now it was a hard obstacle that restricted my lungs and crushed my heart.

When I was able, Joshua led me away from the grisly scene, but mindful of encountering the cultists in the gathering dusk, we did not go far. Without Joshua's support, I dropped my pack and sat, encircled by jungle. Eventually, Joshua made me eat, and, as the food brought me back to myself, I noticed him toying with something.

"What are you doing?" I asked softly. It was the first time either of us had spoken since we found the heads.

He leaned forward, his weathered features exaggerated into deep erosion in the light of our lamps.

"It's what the monkeys were – taking, earlier, by the stream."

"What?"

"The powder – " He offered me the leaf.

What impressed me at first was the simple structure the leaf had been folded into. It had been manipulated to form a secure pouch so cunningly constructed that it may even have been watertight. Not a grain of its sooty contents leaked out.

"This was not made by monkeys," I said. Further evidence of the unseen human inhabitants of the gorge.

I sniffed cautiously, and recognised the sweet odour as similar to that of the bottle I had opened back in the hut, but much stronger. Immediately my head reeled. I almost dropped the pouch.

"It's hallucinogenic," said Joshua. "Like peyote. Something like that." He rose to his feet and stared out into the trees. Then he laughed, and made three quick 'ook' sounds, like a monkey.

"My God, Joshua, have you taken some?"

He fixed my attention with his gaze. His voice was slow, carefully enunciated.

"How else would we know what it was?" He moved his hand in front of my face. The gesture left a trail of hands behind, staccato after-images.

I gasped, startled. Whereas Joshua evidently had experience, I had never explored drugs, prevented from taking such few opportunities as had come my way by the deep fear of surrendering control. But now I had been taken by surprise. As the effects began to intensify, I found them at the same time horrifying and fascinating. I could feel a creeping sensation, like movement, up the sides of my neck, under my jaw then up my face and into my scalp. There was a vague metallic sensation in my nasal cavity, the same taste, perhaps, at the back of my throat.

"Jesus!" It was like being ill, feverish, delirious, but without the lethargy and depression that accompanied such illness.

189

I was still staring at Joshua's face. He, in turn looked intently back at me.

"You're feeling it too, aren't you?" he asked. His voice was drawn out, slightly distorted.

"But I've only smelled it briefly – " His face was moving. Almost imperceptibly, oozing, breathing.

"Imagine what *I* feel like, then," he said, the sensual pulse of movement, as his face twisted, shifting into a grin. Around us the darkness of the jungle began to glow. As I turned my head, everything left a staggered trail of itself. I started to giggle, and immediately stifled it.

Joshua crouched before me.

"Take some," he said. His voice had assumed a new depth, a new breadth of sound.

"What? Are you mad?"

He grasped my wrist. The sensation of his touch was quite alien. He shook his head. "I think you should take some."

"Why? Already I feel – very strange – Joshua, I – "

He leaned close, his face, inches away, was a map of a world I had never seen, but knew of instinctively. Every feature a continent, every wrinkle a tectonic fault. His eyes were the heart of the world, a doorway to something else, to Joshua's private version of Heaven, or Hell.

I stuck two fingers into my mouth, wetting them, and pushed them into the powder.

Joshua's smile widened. "Not too much," he said, and then, bizarrely, added, "the flesh of the *Doorbringer* is powerful stuff."

The soft coating on my fingers, sparkling like black diamond dust captivated me. A night sky in my hand. Thoughts of my son dwindled like a receding star – but did not vanish entirely.

"I can't – " I said, wiping my fingers on my shorts. It seemed some vestige of my normal self remained.

"You can, Andras," Joshua said, simultaneously yanking my head back by the hair, and forcing a fingerful of the grit between my lips. I gagged as he rubbed the stuff roughly around the inside of my cheeks. My mouth rioted with the cold aromatic sweetness. When he released me I tried to spit it out but most of the powder had dissolved. All the same I emptied a water bottle in an effort to dispel the awful taste. As the liquid swirled around my mouth I fell downwards through reality.

The noises of the jungle had become all-encompassing. There was sound everywhere, and further sound within it. Dark layers of deep vibration throbbed out of the darkness, encasing feathery rustles, the movement of creatures among plants, at the edge of hearing the very growth of the plants themselves. The movement echoed the shape of a branch, underlined patches of distant night sky shining through the canopy. As I stared upwards, aware of connections between myself and my environs I had previously been ignorant to (but that somehow were not new to me, were like old friends coming home), the negative and positive inverted, the pieces of sky became the objects, the darkness of the canopy become the void. I felt doors opening all around me. I felt boundaries at the edges of my consciousness dissolve, no longer relevant. The jungle, this reality, I realised, was only a tiny fragment of existence. All things were connected in a framework above and beyond and behind our normal perception.

I got to my feet, stumbled forward, the trees moving aside to create a passage for me. I looked back. Joshua stood beside our tent, far away now. His arms were outstretched in my direction, a gesture of beseeching, and his face was a frieze of abject misery.

Had he spoken? Was that what made me turn? Yes, his lips were moving. I could not quite hear, no – Joshua spoke three syllables in that awful tongue.

Doorbringer, in English, sounded in my mind.

The undergrowth erupted, the very jungle hurtling down from the trees, rising up from the ground, throwing itself upon him. His scream was choked by strong hands as he crumpled under a flailing storm of oddly proportioned limbs.

The attack was timeless, but must have lasted only moments.

191

I watched without emotion as the assailants disengaged from Joshua's ruined corpse, and noticed that they were not after all crazed tribesmen, but simply more apes – perhaps seven individuals – three heavy orangs and four smaller creatures, gibbons, perhaps. Their fur shone blackly, soaked in Joshua's blood. His body lay motionless, hidden behind them. A large orang shuffled towards me, offering a severed arm. One of the gibbons busied itself at Joshua's face and popped a slick, pale sphere into its mouth. I heard it burst between bloodied fangs.

I knew my friend was dead, and that it was my fault for bringing him to this place, but in this state of unreality, it hardly seemed of consequence. It occurred to me he hadn't had time to draw his pistol, and some part of me was telling me I should draw mine, because I was surely next.

But the apes held their ground, swayed there, making noises that resolved into a quiet chant. That word again.

I turned. The avenue of trees had extended, sloping away now into a natural depression in the landscape. At the far end stood the unsteady silhouette of a man framed in front of a dark-lit tower.

Sandor.

By this time any distinction between reality and the effects of the powder had become utterly irrelevant. I could not believe that this was really my son, but the same awful certainty that I knew had guided both of us here in the first place convinced me that it was. The tower was the source of that conviction. The crumbling structure spewed black dust into the glowing sky. Plumes of the stuff drifted across the moon, falling like volcanic ash.

I thought of Sandor's bottles of rain.

The unsolid figure that had once been my son stood before the tower, arms raised in supplication. *Papa*, his voice said in my head, and suddenly I was beside him. *The Doorbringer is giving of its flesh to us.*

A host of apes and monkeys simmered and bubbled into

192

view around us, melting out of the shadows, their faces and bodies echoing about themselves. They leapt and danced as they gathered and ate the powder, scooping it from each other's fur, crying with laughter and epiphanic ecstasy.

The Flesh of the Doorbringer is Truth, the voice of what had been my son sounded in my mind, *The Flesh of the Doorbringer is Release.*

"I don't understand," I said aloud.

Sandor's outline constantly shifted, restless matter fuming under the restrictions of so few dimensions. It regarded me with shadowy orbs where its eyes should have been, and smiled. It gestured at the creatures around us.

These are His worshippers, His people. The Doorbringer does not require worship, but His people do so nevertheless. They raised His tower, crafted artefacts in His honour, to thank Him for giving them intelligence, and language to express it, through the gift of His flesh. They would have killed me, but I had the Key. This. He held up a seething hand, the orange torus gripped within. *Even then I barely made it inside. Oh, oh, what narrow understanding I had then. When first I lay, trapped inside this infernal chimney; to escape the fury of the apes only to die of thirst and hunger within my sanctuary. The passing of days was marked only by the slow traverse of light on the uppermost bricks. But then, as my mortal life ebbed, the moon appeared fat in the chimney mouth, and the Door opened and the Bringer was revealed. He opened my mind and I saw the truth of it.*

"Sandor... what are you saying?" I was shaking. A dark certainty had fallen upon me.

See for yourself.

Sandor approached the tower, and a rectangle of crudely carved wall disappeared. He slipped through it into the darkness within. I hesitated, not at all sure that I had in fact been talking to my son. He didn't talk like Sandor, but there was something in the carriage, the gestures that felt authentic. Certainly all of this had to be part of the hallucination, but if there was any chance that it *was* Sandor then I had to act. As he had ceased to do for me past the age of ten, I followed my son. Into darkness.

At first it was *only* darkness. I was aware of nothing else. Then a sensation, soft like ash landing on my skin, covering me all over despite my clothes. Everywhere the flakes found ingress. They filled me. I felt them blocking my ears and nostrils, damming my eyes, clogging my throat. Suffocating me with darkness. But then the opposite of light shone coldly all around, passing through my flesh and into the depths of my consciousness. Somewhere in my mind, I found a new clarity, enough to understand that I had become engulfed in the Flesh, and had lost all connection with physical reality. The dark-light intensified, and I saw that Sandor and I were floating above a vast plain. It was infinite, empty and full simultaneously, stretching and curling up out of sight, and punctured with myriad portals, doorways, windows, ancient openings into the souls of mankind and a thousand other races. An unseen storm raged in my ears, although I felt not a breath of wind. The source of that sound I could not see anywhere in this bizarre landscape, yet its *presence* was everywhere. The presence had a name. *Doorbringer*.

Doorbringer was feeding. It had been feeding for millennia. Since we swung down out of the trees and onto the plains to brain each other with sticks and rocks, it had thrilled at the expression of the darkness within our souls. As its flesh was a drug to us, so were our sins elixir to it. Its very fabric quivered at the luxurious feast we set.

Dread gripped me as understanding dawned. *Doorbringer* was not a malevolent entity, bringing evil into the hearts of mankind. The evil that it fed upon was ours, and ours alone. *We* were the darkness: we the greedy, the selfish, the angry, the hateful, the ones who turned blind eyes and cold shoulders. Every curse, every hateful bigotry, every shameful blow, every rape, every murder, every ounce of dark pride and shameless arrogance, every life lost through indifference… came from us, not it. We were accountable. There was nothing else to blame. That the creature fed upon us was... coincidental.

The revulsion and longing that I had felt in the torus were my own. No doubt Sandor had had similar experiences, although perhaps less used than I to acknowledging the negativity in himself he had been more easily seduced by it. We were accountable, both for our sins committed and for the potential to commit more. I, however, was ultimately responsible. It was my act that brought us here – brought *him* here. I had delivered the torus into the hands of one sufficiently innocent to be bent completely to the Doorbringer's purpose.

The Truth. You understand, don't you father? You were right all along. Morality is pointless. We are *the darkness. We find it easier to hate than to love.*

The plain vanished. We were in a white place. Hands over my face, I shook and wept. I sobbed and looked up at the face of my son, returned to its fleshly form. A time-stopped mirror. I recalled how as a young man, I had looked into mirrors and seen the face of my own distant father staring back at me. Now I looked at my son, and saw myself.

"I never..." I started to say, but the words wouldn't come. I tasted metal in my mouth.

Sandor crouched, his face drawing closer to mine. Unsteadily, he resumed the restless form of the Doorbringer's Earthly emissary. Points of light, distant moons, shone in his eyes.

Shhh, he said, a finger rising to his lips as he became shadow. *There is only the darkness.*

I closed my eyes. He was right, of course. Oh God. My son. My only child.

Somewhere, I heard rain falling.

Hard To Do

The man on the radio segues with smooth banality into the next request. He tells us, as if we need reminding, that it's a beautiful summer's day and I almost laugh as I recognise the song, turning my attention from the sink to stare at the cheap red boogie box sitting there on the table. The speakers spill those jaunty opening vocals; sugared harmonies as only the Carpenters ever made. The refrain is light and melodic, its message ironically trite. I want to sing along and I want to cry.

Hard to do. Oh yes.

The kettle overflows, cold water flooding over my hands. I place it to one side and return my fingers to the stream. I stand mesmerised by it, the water flashing brightly, drumming into the stainless steel basin, and I enjoy the respite from the sticky hot day until my fingers lose sensation and I start to shiver.

I reach into the drier for a newly laundered towel, and dry my hands with the soft, still-warm fabric. My skin feels caressed.

Neil Williamson

The shiny lid goes back on the kettle, and the whistle cap fits snugly over the spout. I sit at the table to wait. You will be home soon.

*

On the wall, by the phone, hangs that tacky calendar we brought back from Switzerland. Twelve stunningly awful pictures of cows in pastoral Alpine settings. Out of date now, of course, it's a key for memories. I leaf back through the months, reliving shared occasions through scrawled sigils and hieroglyph doodles.

Prior to May, when we bought the thing, the pages are empty. April, March. February has but one date, circled many times, dotted around with red biro love hearts. The first entry you made in it. The day we met. You wouldn't believe how often in the quiet moments when you are not here I have considered the terrifying wonder of the passage of time. Where did the months go? The days, hours, and minutes? The seconds spent just looking at those dumb cows and thinking about this. The ticks in between.

Five hundred days. If the calendar extended this far you would see scratched crosses in black ink marking today's June brightness, desperate lines scoring the paper hard enough to rip through. Looking back after today, I think you might see it like that anyway. Half a thousand days of you. And me.

The kettle boils with a breathy scream, rattling with pent up agitation. I watch it – empathising, feeling the clenching fist tighten in my chest – until it becomes shrill and violent. I snatch it off the hob just in time before... I realise I don't know what would happen if I allowed it to continue.

The water mixes with the jasmine leaf in the little pot. The steam billows in my face as I mix it round with a spoon. If you make it home fast enough it'll be nice and strong, just how you like it.

I like my tea weak – you never did appreciate how weak. I pour myself half a bowl, barely any colour to it, dark leaf bobbing

198

at the bottom. Sitting once more at the table, shifting to avoid the stray piece of wickerwork stabbing into my thigh, I lift the bowl to my face, hold it there, breathing in. Fragrant steam coalesces on my skin. I take a sip, hot and fresh. And I rejoice that I was given this Chinese ancestry, these fine structured features that first attracted you – the delicate bones, the muddy-water eyes.

I love my eyes. You laugh at me for spending so much time looking in the mirror – not making myself up or doing my hair or brushing my teeth, just looking. You've never said, but I know you think I'm vain. How can you mistake vanity for wonder? Wonder at this woman, Julie, who has been fortunate to have loved you. This woman who looks increasingly like a stranger.

I'm beginning to worry that you might not come home, that maybe you'll go to a bar instead, somewhere warm and friendly. Snug, insulated. And maybe you'll just stay there until they slop you out into the darkness because right now you don't want to see me. I can't say I'd blame you, but I hope you come home. Soon, or I'll be gone.

When you get home you'll be impressed. I've tidied up. I've scrubbed the flat from top to bottom; I've cleaned, I've polished. Yes, *really*. It's not something I'm famed for but, well, you've got to try everything once. You won't know the place. It feels almost unlived in.

*

I'm sorry, okay? About the way this has happened. I know it's been hard for you to understand, why things have gone so sour, so fast. I guess it won't be a consolation, but it's harder for me. To see the pain I'm causing you. To turn your words into silence, your approaches to vacuum. To watch you turn in on yourself, quiet and edgy, start up smoking again in some kind of subconscious defiance: and to use that as one more weapon to drive us apart.

Twice I thought you were going to hit me. Some of... *some*

part of me wondered what that would feel like. The anticipation, sickening and exhilarating, the shock cast on your face as, at the last minute, you became aware, watching you fight to control the frustration. Wondering how the dynamics between us would change if you followed through. But you didn't. I was relieved, mostly.

I regret that you'll end up feeling this way about me. Bad, I mean. But hopefully you won't feel inclined to try and find me after I'm gone. We thought it would be best this way – you'll have others, you shouldn't miss out on them, chasing after someone you will never find again. I envy you the complexity of what you feel.

*

I find I'm humming along to a new tune, although the radio has gone quiet. It has the same fluffy addictiveness as the song that was on earlier. The Carpenters again, that's right. I remember how we used to go out driving just so we could blast this stuff out of the stereo and sing our guts out. I wish we could do that again, just once more. I let the melody run its course, dredging up some words to go with it.

Why do birds....?

While I was tidying I found a new pack of Silk Cut. I've placed it with your Atlanta Braves ashtray and a cheap plastic lighter at the centre of the table. The strip tears easily, the wrapping sloughs off like cellophane skin. I remove one cigarette, hold it between my fingers. Its lightness is frightening. This is all the weight you attach to your life. And you wonder why it angers me. The hate I feel when you light up is the strongest passion I have.

Some of us don't have so long. We appreciate each and every of our days, and we waste none of our time.

A band of sunlight enfolds my arm, makes the skin glow, illuminating the tiny dark hairs, but I no longer feel the sensation of warmth that should accompany it. Involuntarily, I shiver. I don't feel cold, though. We don't feel anything.

I spark the gas, bring the small flame close to the palm of my hand. Closer, almost touching. Thankful, I feel heat, sharpening to a red point of pain. I move the lighter to the cigarette, watch as the tip glows, blackens. Carefully I lay it down in the centre of the clean ashtray and watch it gradually turn to ash. The smoke catches in my throat, brings a dull throb to my temple.

We've forgotten what colour your hair is. Your eyes, yes, there is a clear picture, blue discs, slivers of sky – but your hair, it's dark isn't it, or perhaps more a sandy red. I'll know soon when you return from ... from that place where you spend the days.

I wait, feeling increasingly,... *detached*. The cigarette has burned all the way to the filter, a slender cylinder of ash.

I dip a finger in my tea, try hard to stamp the feeling on my memory. I smudge the soft tube with the moist finger. Gritty speckled grey, coating my skin. I place it in my mouth, lick the flaky powder. It tastes like death and chokes me. Tears in my eyes, I swig my tea to rinse my mouth. I forget the taste of the ash, I forget the taste of the tea. I dip my finger and scoop some more, smearing it around the inside of my cheeks and gums. I pop the papery filter, nasty medicine for a terminal case.

We know we are losing it. It was inevitable, but that doesn't make it any easier.

*

"What are you doing?"

The voice is familiar, the face too – round, lined with concern. The eyes we recognise. The hair, after all, is dark brown.

You come and sit by me at the table, taking my trembling hand and ask, "What's wrong?"

I can see that you are already halfway to interpreting the situation for yourself. You sense an end to things, you feel that this is where we break up. In this instant you hate me for making this happen; and for the small feeling of guilt rising with the realisation that you are not as upset as you feel you ought to be.

I can't remember your name. My own was never important, but losing yours is tragic. Tears, again.

*

The second time around, sharing a shortened life with a million others, the experience is less immediate, diluted – like viewing it all through dirty glass – but at the same time infinitely more wonderful. The second time around, tears are always an occasion for joy. The colour orange is a miracle. The deep, dizzy smell of mimosa and the polyglot dialects of music: from the heart-stopping slow grief of Gorecki right through to the superficiality of the packaged pop voices of Richard and Karen. All of it is to be treasured with joy and with regret that we never appreciate anything fully the first time when it is all new and we have our own single set of totally devoted senses to comprehend it.

In a minute or so you will have talked to me (although we won't have answered), tried to hold me (like melting ice), and watched me lift a suitcase (which does not exist) and walk out of our lives.

During that minute *we* will strip down into brittle ribbons, thin as parchment and fly, whipping and twisting, into the never, disintegrating to dust. Billows of saffron, glinting hails of carnelian and jade. Soul pollen, we mix and float on the breath of the world, aware of nothing but the longing for our five hundred days to come again.

The Codsman and His Willing Shag

Old Peter had a way of looking at a pint that gave the impression that his world started and ended at those foam-flecked glass walls. A sailor he was, adrift on a murky, hand-pulled, real-ale sea. He had the look of a Crusoe about him anyway: all that wildman grey hair and beard, the chunky Arran-knit sweater, nicotine-stained around the collar. Of course, the nautical look was part of the band's image, but Peter really lived it. It was in his eyes, that impression that he was staring at a different horizon from everyone else.

Damien sipped his cider and pulled himself back into the nook, partly to avoid any awkward questions about his age and partly in case any of the guys from school – Mark McGregor and his year six crowd, who didn't bat an eye at drinking in The Dolphin even though they weren't much older than him – came in. Damien hadn't gone as far as the full beard, but the band had encouraged the bushy sideburns, and McGregor's lot hadn't been slow to notice. He didn't really care what they thought of him, but he could do without the oh-so-witty shouts of 'Oi, Supergrass.' He tugged the itchy wool of his own pristine sweater away from his neck and gulped his cider.

Peter looked up from his glass, raising a nimbus eyebrow. "You'll be wanting another in a minute," he said. It didn't seem to be a question.

This was getting really awkward.

For the next few minutes they both drank in silence, but when Peter started humming a tune, drumming his fingers on the sticky table top, Damien couldn't take it any longer.

"Rodger's sacking Steve, isn't he?"

Peter shrugged. "The lad's a fine guitar player," he said, "but he's got ideas that aren't right for Smuggler's Knot."

Damien sank back. He had known it from the look on Rodger's face when Steve had accidentally chopped a little groove into *The Eddystone Light*. Then when the group's leader had offered to help Steve load his gear into the car, and suggested none too subtly that Damien stay behind for a post-gig drink with Peter instead of Steve giving him a lift home as usual ... well it was too obvious wasn't it. Rodger. He might have been one of his dad's mates, but ... *what a prick.*

"Steve's a better musician than all of us put together," Damien said. "Where's Rodger think we're going to find another guitarist that good. Robin Hood's Bay's hardly swarming with them." Robin Hood's Bay was hardly swarming with *anything* apart from smugglers tales and misplaced tourists.

Peter appeared unaffected by Damien's outburst. "Shanty scores say *trad.* on them," he said patiently, as if explaining the bleeding obvious to a five-year-old. "So they should be played trad." He nodded at the glass in Damien's hand. "I'll get them in then, I suppose."

Well it's not like they'll serve me, is it? thought Damien as he watched Peter at the bar, fishing coins out of a grubby purse. He checked the door too, in case any of McGregor's lot did put in

The Codsman and His Willing Shag

an appearance. Maybe if just Heather Burnett came in it wouldn't be so bad to be spotted having a couple of pints – even with someone as terminally uncool as Peter – but the door stayed firmly shut.

While he waited, Damien became aware of a tune in his head. One of the shanties. God, they'd not played that one in ages: *The Codsman And His Willing Shag*. The first verse rolled through his mind.

> *A Codsman he went out to sea*
> *And left his lovely, dawn til eve*
> *And pine she did for company*
> *And suitors had she many.*

What had put that into his head? It was one of those bawdy ballads that went down well with rugby clubs and the like, but it had been months since they'd played to more than a handful of the Dolphin's salty regulars. This time of year with the tourists away, it was a ghost town, this place. Especially when your only means of escape was the shitty bus service or cadging a lift off your parents.

Steve was bloody lucky to have a car, but Damien was going to miss more than the lifts home: he'd miss their chats too, when even the act of driving along to a guilty indie soundtrack, and talking about Steve's acceptance to Leeds University, had felt like a vicarious taste of freedom. Rodger didn't know that Steve had been going to leave anyway, but it wouldn't have been a surprise. Everyone left here as soon as they were able. Damien himself would be learning to drive in a year's time. He couldn't wait.

He looked up at the sound of Peter singing.

> *But she turned her back on each dandy cock*
> *And she waited day long on her rock*
> *Til the Codsman sailed back home to her*
> *Til the Codsman sailed back home.*

Neil Williamson

Oh please. It was a jaunty wee tune, even in Peter's bassy growl, but it was bad enough singing it as part of their set without calling attention to themselves in the pub. "Drink up," the older man said, sitting down and taking a long swig from his own glass. Damien looked warily at the new pint sitting beside the one had yet to finish. He stifled a burp. If he wasn't careful he was going to get pissed.

"Shouldn't be in too much of a hurry to leave your roots behind, son," Peter said. "You think there's so much more to be had in Scarborough or Leeds, London even? Maybe so, but a place like this, *your home town*, it's in your skin. A place like this has got things you'll not find anywhere else, no matter how far you go."

How would you know? Damien thought, but didn't say. He liked Peter, especially as an alternative to talking to Rodger. He genuinely admired the old man's musical knowledge, but he was a fixture of the town. What did he know of the rest of the world?

"Nowhere else has rain?" Damien didn't bother to keep the sarcasm out of his voice. "Nowhere else has gloomy black slate? Slippery cobbled hills? Half-dead pubs?"

Peter grinned into his glass. "Nowhere else has traditions," he patted the accordion on the seat next to him. "Not like *our* traditions."

"Are you talking about the shanties?" Damien asked. "They're just stupid old songs."

There might have been a flicker of anger in the way that Peter smacked down his already nearly empty pint glass, but it didn't enter his rumbling drawl. "Drink up, son, I've got something to show you."

When they left the pub ten minutes later, the weather conspired with the hastily downed cider to remind Damien of what he was so anxious to leave behind. The wind slapped him with a fistful of rain just as his first lungful of cold air rushed to his head. Dizzy for a second, he leaned against the wet brick, and

206

The Codsman and His Willing Shag

watched Peter arch his back and suck the squall into his puffed out chest.

"I have to get the last bus," Damien murmured, surprised at how slurred the words came out. He'd got drunk with friends tons of times, but never this fast. Even as he thought about catching the absurdly early last bus for Whitby that would drop him at his road end on the edge of town, he began to wonder if the long, bracing walk up the hill wouldn't be a better plan. He might even be nearly sober by the time his mum saw him.

"Come on." Peter led him down the steep and slick-stoned street. A gaggle of misplaced tourists hurried past them, a cloud of laughter erupting like sea spray from their midst.

You live in a small town all your life, you know it intimately. Its streets are as familiar as the rooms of your own house, its buildings, your wallpaper. The tang of brine is the smell of your mother's cooking, and the constant conversation of sea and wind and gulls, the muted, ever-present soundtrack of domestic appliances. It's always the same. You stop thinking of it as a place. You stop thinking about it at all.

There was a shut-up shop not far down the hill that had appeared surreptitiously like a patch of damp on the bathroom ceiling. Damien couldn't remember it ever being open, or what had been there before, but for years now it had been an unmovable stain on Robin Hood's Bay's decor. Its window displayed a sparse diorama of oddments. Dusty figurines of dolphins and starfish sat on a fan of garish guidebooks. There was other statuary too, dragons and goblins, perhaps a misguided attempt at snagging some of Whitby's Goth trade, sat opposite a collection of cutesy animal figures; kittens in mittens, frogs with fishing rods. It was no wonder the shop had gone bust.

It was a surprise however when Peter stopped there and pulled out a set of keys. "You wouldn't believe how cheap the rent is," he said, opening the door with his shoulder. "Course its only short term until they find a new tenant for the shop." He

207

stepped through the darkened doorway, and Damien was only able to surmise the grin in his voice. "Been here four years now."

There was a little flat to the rear of the empty sales space. Peter and Damien squeezed down a hall and a twist of carpeted stairs until they arrived at a cramped little kitchen that clearly hadn't been decorated since the sixties. Peter laid down his instrument. Damien did the same and, while the old man left the room for a moment, took the opportunity to look around. He found he was surprised by how tidy Peter kept the place, and then he was ashamed that he'd assumed that an older man living on his own would have piles of crusty dishes in the sink and unwashed floors. There wasn't much to this kitchen, but what there was was neatly stowed. The economy of space reminded Damien of the cabin of a boat, and he wondered if, unlike the rest of the Knot, Peter did in fact have actual seafaring credentials.

Peter returned with two glasses, and a bottle which Damien eyed warily. It had no label and looked as if it had been retrieved from the depths of a dusty cupboard. Peter indicated that he should sit, and settling himself on the opposite side of the table, removed the bottle's roughly shaped cork.

"What's this?" After their short walk Damien had got over the wooziness brought on by the cider, and he wasn't especially keen to reprise the feeling right away.

"Taste of home." Oblivious to Damien's nervousness, Peter poured a small measure into the glasses. The liquid could have been water, except that it had the palest of greenish tinges to it. Or was it bluish? In the electric light it was impossible to tell. "It's called *scouridge*. Taste-wise, the closest thing to it, you might say, would be an Islay whisky, but it's much better than that." He picked up one of the glasses and nudged the other towards Damien.

Damien didn't know where Islay was, or how its flavour might differ from normal Scotch, but his one taste of his dad's Bells last New Year hadn't enamoured him to the drink. He remembered: it had been Rodger that had brought the bottle to

The Codsman and His Willing Shag

Damien's parents' house, and Peter had turned down the offered glass with a barely concealed disregard that had pissed Rodger off. Now, while he liked the idea of Dad's friends treating him at last like an adult, and he didn't want to offend Peter the same way, he didn't have an awful lot of experience with spirits, and he'd already had two pints. Then again, there was barely a quarter of an inch of the stuff in the tumbler. He should be able to swallow that down for politeness' sake. He picked up the glass and a powerful smell hit him, a complex aroma that reminded him of a dozen things all at once: wet shingle and kelp and winkle shells and sea grasses and scurrying white feathers and flying his kite in the blustering wind up on the cliffs, and...

Damien put his glass down in surprise.

Peter was watching him. "Familiar, isn't it?" he said. "You see? You do know your home. I told you, it's in your skin. Same as the shanties, son. They might not look like much more than a bit of fun and fancy on the surface, but many of them are based on old stories. Take our Codsman for example, now."

Damien almost laughed out loud. *The Codsman* was as silly as they came, a ridiculous fabrication about a jilted fisherman's wife who waited and waited for her husband to return, spurning the advances of the other men of the town. The professions of these men had apparently been chosen by the *double entendres* they offered.

Well the tailor came to press his suit
And to offer her his needle
But her dress was flattened by the wind
And his ardour by her thimble

Damien shook his head. He'd learned in History how facts got stretched and inflated by posterity. "Come on," he said, "if *The Codsman* is based on a true story, it's nothing more than a woman whose husband ran away. All that stuff about the butcher and the baker and the lampwick was just added to make it funny."

209

Peter shrugged. "You think so?"

"Sure. It's not even that great a song. Even we don't play it very often."

"It's not the catchiest of tunes, I'll grant you that, son." Peter seemed to be hiding a smile in his beard. "But the audiences do like to join in with the chorus."

"Only because they get to shout the word 'cock' in a public place."

Peter actually did laugh at this, and Damien tried not to feel that he was the subject of his amusement. Maybe Peter spotted this, because he raised his glass of scouridge. "Drink up, Damien," he said, and tossed the pale alcohol back.

Damien brought the glass up to his lips. That smell again, the slipping of shale, the feel of wet rock and limpets under his bare feet. He took a sip. It was cold, slightly oily, but tasted of nothing. The drink was all aroma. Damien pinched his nose and drained his glass. *Easy.*

A second later cold fire uncoiled in his belly, reached up into his throat. Damien suppressed the urge to gag, but after another second it had withdrawn, settling choppily in his stomach.

"All right?" Peter was already pouring them both another shot.

Damien nodded, not trusting his ability to speak while his tongue still tingled with the medicinal tang. His mouth felt like a shoreline cave, recently sluiced by the high tide. He bet that, for all their cool and their boasting, none of McGregor's clique ever drank anything like scouridge. In fact, for all their talk, they likely hadn't actually drunk in the Dolphin more than a handful of times. Right now McGregor and Heather and the rest were probably in someone's bedroom passing round a bottle of vodka.

"Place like this," Peter said, "a place built with discretion in mind, is good at keeping its secrets, son."

"You mean all the smuggler stuff?" Like any kid who went to school in these parts Damien knew all about it. That the village had reputedly been scraped out of the cliff face in such an

The Codsman and His Willing Shag

inaccessible location because it afforded excellent opportunities to avoid the local excise men. That the town was said to be riddled with passages that allowed travel between houses without using the public streets. And true enough, he had heard that some of the older houses had cemented-over trap doors in kitchen floors and bricked-up doorways in cellars. But all of that had been investigated and documented – the gift shops were well stocked with thin volumes by amateur historians. It wasn't what you'd call secret.

A second glass of scouridge was nudged towards him. Damien watched the liquid slosh and caught a brief whiff of it, and this time remembered a feeling. It was the feeling of being thrilled by the mystery of the world. He remembered, not so many years ago, when he had been eight or nine and had been allowed for the first time to wander a little farther from home, he had spent the summer afternoons exploring the old parts of town. Every weathered house had a secret cellar that housed a smugglers' den. Every oddly regular pattern of bricks was a secret door that, if he could press the right sequence, would open a tunnel to a cave filled with forgotten contraband. Every cliff path was a potential route to a concealed cove, and a rotted jetty with rowing boats still tied up, waiting for a clipper to drop anchor at night and a coded sequence of lights to be issued in the darkness.

The feeling he remembered was the potential for magic as he explored every corner for the first time on his own. But that sensation of adventure had waned as Damien had become familiar with his town. Familiarity had bred boredom, then indifference; the contempt was a relatively recent emotion that had come with a teenager's increasing, frustrated awareness of the wider world.

"But there's more to our traditions than the smuggling," Peter went on. "The men round here have always gone to sea, son. They always go, and they always come home. Their hearts draw them back. That's what our sea songs are about. Going out and coming home."

211

Neil Williamson

Damien thought about that. True that a lot of songs the Knot sang had something of that at their centres – not the popular, well-known ones that all the other bands sang, but the esoteric ones of which Rodger and Peter seemed to have a never-ending supply. More than once Steve had confided that he thought the two senior members had made them up themselves. In these songs the sea was life's great unknown. Man's relationship with it involved forging a path outwards from land, and always ended with a homeward trip. Sailors voyaging to the new world returned with exotic promise, rescuers dashing out in storms came back either as heroes or ghosts, and fishermen forged the same path daily to keep their families fed and clothed. Nevertheless, he could think of an obvious counter-example to Peter's theory.

"What about *The Codsman*?" he said.

"What about it?"

"Well, he doesn't come back home does he? The wife waits for him to come home but he never does."

Peter grinned. "Ah, but are you sure you know the whole song?"

Damien regarded him, genuinely surprised.

"See Damien, son, there's more to that song than we normally sing. After all the fun of the rest of the song, it's a bit of a downer as you might say." He bent down, snapped his accordion out of its case and hitched it over his shoulders. Damien watched the older man's rough, raw fingers dance over the keys as he played the boisterously familiar melody and crooned the opening of the song's final verse.

"Well, the lampwick came to bring her light, and to bring her comfort in the night." Peter stopped playing. "You know this far, yes?"

Damien nodded.

"Well, this is what follows." He quickly ripped through the rest of the verse and fast-forwarded through the rollickingly saucy chorus that followed, as if it weren't after all the most important

212

The Codsman and His Willing Shag

Peter after all? But the rough shove didn't come. He wasn't sent sprawling onto the stone floor, imprisoned in sudden darkness. And when he turned to look, Peter hadn't turned into some depraved monster.

"Just find your way down to the end, Damien," the old man said gently. "And come back up when you're ready. I'll leave the door open."

In the end it was the darkness that drew him, ducking, through the door; *the unknown*, that thrill of mystery that he had not experienced since he was a kid.

The cellar was not a cellar, but a passage. It didn't take long, with all the kinks and dog-legs to leave behind the light from Peter's kitchen, but Damien allowed the cold walls to guide him. The walls, and his imagination.

It was a proper smugglers' tunnel, finished without finesse, where it was finished at all. The further stairs he encountered, leading down, always down, were little more than shelves hacked out of the rock. The steeper sections had rusted cleats and the rotten remains of old rope hand rails. The wider sections had rough pens for stacking barrels and crates. A trick of the acoustics modulated the echoes of his own footsteps into urgent piratical conversation, either in the tunnel just ahead of him or where he had just been, that stopped as soon as he stopped to listen.

The further down he went, the damper the walls became, and the louder came the sound of the waves. And it was no surprise when he stepped out of a cleft between angled strata of rock onto a thin wedge of beach.

His heart spun gloriously, like he had finally worked out the combination of bricks to open the secret door.

There was little here but the rocks and the shingle, and the patient waves that had come and were now retreating, leaving the beach glittering under the moon. From somewhere nearby there came a chatter of bird call – *ka-ka-kaak* – not a sound of alarm, but a curious domestic noise that made Damien feel as if he were eavesdropping outside someone's house. There was something else on the beach too. A dark mass spread across the shingle. At first he thought it was weed, but it did not glisten the way kelp or wrack would. He bent down – *feathers*. A drift of feathers. He picked one up. It was long and black as oil, with a green sheen that revealed itself as he spun it between his fingers.

This was a magical place right enough. A rarely disturbed secret place. *A heart*. It wasn't what he would have wanted to find when he was a kid – there was no jetty, no boats, no smugglers' treasure – but why should his childish fantasies have anything to do with the reality of the town's secret centre?

Ka-ka-kaak. Those gulls again. And closer by, a lower, gruffer sound like a cough and a groan. Damien peered into the darkness, where the shapes of the rock met the rhythmic shimmer of the water.

One of the shapes moved, or the moonlight moved across it, or ... no, it moved. It rose, it stretched. Slim shoulders flexed, and once identified as shoulders Damien connected them to the sweep of a spine, a full curve of buttock, legs tucked underneath. The pose was instantly reminiscent of a classical mermaid, or an advert for shampoo, and would have been incongruous in this place had it not been for the pitchy lustre of the skin, as dark as the night and the water, and for the great wings that extended finally with that flexing of the shoulders.

And, at last, for the head, that took an age to slink around on its goosey neck and fix Damien with such a look. It was a woman's face, of course – the eyes white and wide with outrage or loss, or perhaps just incomprehension – but the forlorn sounds that issued from it were not. The empty clack of the long, hooked bill preceded a very human sigh that became a deep, corvine *chuff*, and a long, frustrated wail.

Then she – it – folded her wings in, and turned her back on him, facing out towards the sea once more, and Damien lost her in the gloom again.

The journey back to Peter's kitchen was a blur of frustration. After that initial glimpse, all he wanted was to stay on the beach and see her again, but there had been such a clear note of dismissal in her turning away that he felt compelled to leave. In the passage, that dismissal was a pressure at his back that propelled him like water in a pipe until he emerged, breathless, into the electric light and the solid reality of the kitchen.

In Damien's absence Peter appeared to have done little except tidy away the scouridge bottle and put the kettle on. The earthy stink of fresh coffee flooded into him, swamping the last vestiges of salt and sea, and with the cellar door shut again, the entire experience shifted and became like a dream.

"Thought you might want a little sober-me-up before you go home to your mum," Peter said when Damien sat down. It was clear he wasn't going to say anything about the beach, and Damien realised that he was relieved. It was his own thing, and he didn't want to dilute it by sharing it.

"What's this?" he asked, indicating the book that Peter had been flipping through when he returned.

"It's called an *atlas*, son. What do they teach you in school these days?" The habitual grin within the beard told him the sarcasm wasn't real. Peter spread the book open at a map of the world. The paper was pocked all over with black ink crosses, and the oceans and seas were filled with cramped notes that spilled into the margins as if to say that the world wasn't big enough for all of Peter's travels.

"Thought you might be interested in how far you can go," he said, "before you need to come home again."

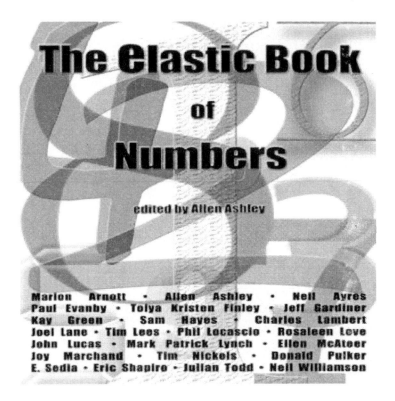

The Elastic Book of Numbers
Available Now From Elastic Press

Numbers rule our lives: clocks, calendars and deadlines; salaries and benefits; tax codes and pin numbers; mortgages, bills and credit limits; the FTSE and the Dow Jones; mobiles, land lines and pagers; binary strings of digitised information held for and about us, instantly accessible.

In this unique collection of 21 stories, some of the world's finest fictioneers examine the effect of numbers on humankind's past, present and future. From the rewriting of history through the thrill of the roulette wheel to the codes controlling the starships, each of these tales engages with numbers in innovative, entertaining and meaningful ways.

www.elasticpress.com